CONOR

THE O'FARRELL BROTHERS

BOOK 1

KATE BONHAM

Cover Design by Wingfield Designs

Editing by Ravenna Poe Edits

Formatting by Author Mojo

ISBN (Print): 978-0-6456537-2-4

MIDNIGHT DREARY
PUBLISHING

This book is for those who love Irish men,
mafia and fiery redheads.

PLAYLIST

The Most Beautiful Girl in the World – Prince

Only Wanna Be with You – Hootie & the Blowfish

Alive – Pearl Jam

If You Could Only See – Tonic

The World I Know – Collective Soul

Dreams – The Cranberries

Disappear – INXS

Bulletproof – La Roux

Don't Blame Me – Taylor Swift

CHAPTER ONE

CONOR

I closed the blinds on my makeshift office at the docks and sat back down at my desk, pouring myself another whiskey. It had been a fucking long day. My brothers had been down my throat about the split of our control in the city yet again. Being the youngest son of the old mob boss, Finneas, I had always had a lot to prove. My older brothers Lorcan and Killian had always been my father's pride and joy. When dad died, we'd split the job of controlling the empire in Ireland. I had gotten the docks, guns and protection of businesses loyal to my father. It was me that put my boots through the glass windows when they didn't pay on time. It was me who had to prove more than my older brothers because they had been raised to take over, whereas I had been the baby. The one they didn't think could handle my shit.

But they had been wrong. Within a few months I had taken control of my part of Ireland and now no one disrespected me. But I also didn't give in to my brothers' demands to know every little thing about my side of the business.

I downed the rest of my drink and poured myself another. The door to my office burst open and my boys Jye and Marcus walked in. They dropped the bag full of protection money on the desk, but I could already tell it wasn't everything.

"That looks light."

"It is, by about four grand."

I looked up at Jye, downing my drink quickly, the burn of the whiskey warming me, before I got up.

"What the fuck happened?"

Marcus came forward. "There appears to be a rebellion rising against you and your brothers. As far as I can see, it's started with Paul O'Reilly and has gathered steam with Peter Kennedy."

I knew Peter, he was a weakling and would never lead anyone to doing something to piss me off. He had owed his life to my father once upon a time. Paul had to be the real leader. I hated that fucking guy. He had butted heads with our family for as long as I could remember. A feud that went down the generations from the start and carried through to me and Paul's sons now.

"Come on," I said to them. "We're going to pay him a little visit."

Jye and Marcus followed me out of the office and toward my car. I got in behind the wheel and sped us down the streets of Galway toward the shop I knew the Kennedy's had run for decades. They were situated near the bay and were some of the oldest shops in the city. Jye pulled our guns out from under the seat and loaded them. As I pulled up outside their shops, I saw the light on in Peter's convenience shop. Jye handed me my gun and I put it into my belt, under my jacket. I made a move to open the door but it was locked.

Marcus smashed his leg through the glass and unlocked it from the inside. Paul and Peter came running out, only to back up when they saw me. Peter looked like a kid with his hand caught in the cookie jar. He was defiant, and I knew instantly he would be the reason I lost my cool and shot up the shops we were supposed to protect. Fuck me, he reminded me of the old school professor that I hated.

"I'm here for my money," I said, looking over at the two of them. "I've heard you are but a few refusing to pay this week."

"We're sick of you and your demands for money" Paul spat viciously. "We're not paying."

"Oh really?" I aimed at him, as he approached me. He stayed well enough away that I couldn't reach him, but I could see he was trying to keep a solid foot away from me. I had to give him props, not many dared to defy me or my brothers.

"Now get out," Paul said. Peter still hadn't said a thing to me. I looked over at him, cowering behind his counter.

"I don't think so," I said. "When I came to you and told you what I could protect you from, you eagerly agreed to pay me weekly for our services. Why are you now refusing to pay?"

"We had an agreement with your father," Paul said. "Not with you or your demented spawn of Satan brothers."

I smiled at the moniker for my brothers. "Spawn of Satan? I guess that's one way to describe them. Do you really want to piss them off?"

"Here," I heard Peter say from behind the counter. He opened his register and threw money on the ground. Jye bent to pick it all up. "I'll give you the rest next week."

I turned back to Paul who looked disappointed in Peter. I could sense a stern talking to about pride after we left.

"I expect money next week, Paul."

"Or what?"

I pulled my gun out of my belt and took aim at Paul's feet, shooting into the center of his foot. Blood spilled out over the floor instantly as he clutched at his foot.

"Don't test me, O'Reilly," I said. Jye and Marcus both headed out the broken door and I continued after them, just as a woman headed toward us. I looked over at her, blindsided by her beauty. Her beautiful red hair was down, curling around her shoulders. Even in the dark, I could tell she had beautiful green eyes and freckles over her nose but not too much, the kind of freckling all the girls wanted these days.

"What the fuck is going on?" she aimed toward me. Jye was about to push her away and warn her but I held my arm out to stop him. "What the fuck did you do to me da's shop?"

"Peter's your father?"

"Now that we're acquainted, how about you tell me who the fuck you are?"

Peter ran out and grabbed hold of his wild eyed daughter and tried to pull her away from me. "I'm sorry, Conor, she's got her mother's fire."

"I can see that."

She made a move to get free of her father's grip to have a go at me, but he wheeled her around and shoved her into the shop.

I couldn't do anything but laugh as Jye started the car. I'd never had any woman dare to challenge me like that and honestly, it was titillating.

As I got in the car, I couldn't help but notice how my

body felt like it was tingling all over. It took everything in me not to march back in there and grab her, take her over my shoulder and carry her off to my apartment for a night of spanking. My cock was at full attention behind my jeans just thinking about all the things I could do to that mouth.

"Where to, boss?" Jye asked, a tight smirk on his lips. He knew I was suffering from a major cockus erectus behind my jeans right now.

"Home. I need to get to the club tonight. Killian's having some sort of conniption about his security."

Jye nodded and drove toward my apartment. Peter's daughter was still very much on my mind.

TEEGHAN

"TEEGHAN," my father said angrily as he turned on me once we were inside the shop. I could hear Paul groaning in the background but I didn't take my eyes off my father. "You do not speak to Conor O'Farrell like that."

"O'Farrell?" I repeated.

"Yes, the O'Farrell's. He is the youngest brother."

"Why was he here smashing up the shop, da?"

My father looked away from me and instantly I knew he had done something stupid. I knew who the O'Farrell's were but I didn't know they had a brother called Conor or that he was drop dead sexy. When he had smirked at me after I swore at him, my insides did a little flip thing and butterflies exploded throughout my stomach. I hadn't had that feeling in years, probably over a decade now and definitely not since my divorce.

"What did you do?"

"Nothing," I heard Paul say a little breathless behind

5

me. I hated that fucking guy. He was always conning my father into doing something stupid. "Now, Peter, where is that fucking ambulance?"

Finally, I turned around to see him on the floor, his foot wrapped in red, bloody rags. I fought off the smile I could feel coming. Instantly, I felt something like admiration for Conor for doing to Paul what I could only dream of doing.

My father ran off to call the ambulance and I looked out over at the door, the glass was completely smashed. We'd have to board that door up so nothing else happens to the shop. I made a move to head into the back to grab some plywood, and I moved a little too close to Paul, faking a trip over his injured foot. He screamed out in pain and grabbed at his foot while I apologized, trying not to laugh at the blunder.

"Teeghan."

My father was not impressed but I was thoroughly amused and that was all that mattered. As I grabbed the pieces of plywood, I dragged them through the store and toward the front door. Since I'd been back in Ireland, I had been helping my father's business with his books. Since my mother died, he'd been relying on the help of some kind souls but now I was here to do it and I could see he didn't have the money to pay for a new door.

His business was close to being bankrupt if he didn't get customers and soon but if they saw a door like this, busted up, they would assume he was dealing with Conor and not on the good side of dealing with him. They'll never cross an O'Farrell. We were all told never to cross the 'O's' as they were called and for the most part, we never saw them.

Until tonight, that is.

God, why couldn't I get Conor's delectable smirk out of my mind?

The sounds of the ambulance coming toward the shop could be heard outside. I grabbed my keys.

"I'll head off now."

My father waved at me to leave, and I walked down to my car parked down the street and got in. I was counting the days before I returned to London after my divorce. Of course my ex would still be in the city but it was big enough I'd probably never run into him or his young, hot and sweet new fiancée, Emma. My now ex-best friend from London.

The thought of running into them was a little devastating but it was nothing compared to being stuck in Ireland for the rest of my life.

I'd had nothing but heartbreak here.

Onwards and upwards as my ma would always say but the way my father flitted around Paul worried me.

I may just have to stay long enough to free him from whatever hold the O'Reilly's had on him.

CHAPTER TWO

CONOR

We sat in the car on the opposite side of the docks. I hated waiting, and everyone knew it. In recent days, I'd become aware of a seller trying to offload his weapons to potential buyers. No one even dared to buy from anyone but me in Ireland which this seller was starting to understand so I had offered to meet with him and negotiate a price for his weapons. I had a feeling they were hot but I couldn't just tell him no. There was always some idiot wanting to make a name for themselves by going against us. I usually never came to these meets, it was a tedious business having to deal with idiots selling their guns to us. Tonight, they'd only agreed to sell to us if I came. My reputation has preceded me, it seems. Jye, and my two enforcers Jakob and Luke, sat in the car with me. I fiddled with my phone, flicking through the messages of naked women. I had no idea why but these women always wanted to send me their naked photos, as if that would entice me into their beds. Sure, they were nice to look at but it took a lot more than a few filtered photos to get me hard enough to want to do something about it.

"Where the fuck are they?" Luke exploded. He'd not wanted to come tonight. I knew the reason had nothing to do with what we did, but more the fact that he and his wife had been arguing lately about his involvement with our crew. She'd never liked me and she made that perfectly clear every time I saw her.

"He's late, we should leave," Jakob said. He had about the same amount of patience as I did. It's why I liked having him around. He was a no bullshit kind of guy. Jye had a lot more patience than I did, so he calmed me down when I needed it.

"Give him five more minutes," Jye offered. "This could make or break us on the guns, not to mention we could find out who his dealer is."

"We'll see," I told him.

It was at that moment, we saw the headlights of another car in the abandoned car park. Here we go.

"We're on," Jye said, getting out of the car first. The rest of us followed suit. I looked over at the fucker who had brought guns into my town. He really thought he could succeed here without my approval? When he realized no one would buy off anyone but me, he knew he had to sell to me. This was going to be one hell of a negotiation.

"I don't like this," I heard Jakob say. "He's brought one car, he can't possibly have that many guns in there."

He had a point. I looked to see if there was a van parked somewhere close by but it did look as if there were only one car. Before I could reach them, Jakob pushed me down so I was covered by the car door. He took cover and drew his weapon. Shots started to ring out, coming from them and from us. I looked everywhere for somewhere to aim. My gun was in my hand, instinctively.

"Shit," I heard Jye mumble from somewhere near me.

"What is it?" I ask.

"They got Luke."

I looked over to where Luke had been standing, only he was now lying on the ground, a big hole in his head. His eyes wide open.

Fuck.

I tried to look for an exit, but they had driven into the spot where we would need to go to get out. We needed to split up and run back to our side of the docks. We would have a cache of guns there, no one would be stupid enough to invade us on our home turf. Hell, this was brazen though. I had to give them props for trying to take me out here.

I was going to kill these motherfuckers. My anger swept over me, for Luke, for the disrespect. My phone was still in the car, I couldn't call for reinforcements.

Jye and I heard footsteps approaching and we jumped up, covering our bodies with the open car door and taking aim. We shot at the two men who had been looking for our dead bodies. They fell, blood spurting out of their bodies. One tried to pull himself to safety before I took a shot at his neck. Blood exploded out of him and he stopped moving.

The sound of a car reversing had us moving away from the other car, only to have the leader running scared and trying to get into the car. He left the bodies of his fallen comrades.

I felt the rage surge within my body at the fact he thought he could fuck me over. No one messes with the O'Farrell's.

"Get Luke," I ordered. Jye ran over to him, pulling him up. Jakob helped carry him back to the car. They put him in the back, Jye sitting next to him before I jumped in the front and we took off back to the office on the other side of the docks. I needed to find this cocksucker and make him pay. I slammed on the brakes once we got back to the office.

"Jake, I need you to speak to his wife," I told him. "She knows you better than us."

"On it."

He got out of the car and took off to his own car. Hopefully Jakob could help to calm the rage I knew would be directed at me for her husband's death. It was a solid chance he could, he was one of the best at doing that but if they had been fighting before he came tonight, god only knew the reaction she would have at never being able to say she was sorry. I just didn't want her to do anything stupid like go to the cops. We owned the cops. We knew about every single complaint or threat against us, so it would be foolish but I also understood grieving women.

They weren't to be messed with.

"Jye, I need you to tell me everything you know about this seller."

"We need to get the body to the morgue," he said.

"I'll take it," I said. "It's on the way to the estate. I need to call a family meeting."

Jye nodded and headed back to the office. I slammed on the accelerator and headed into the city, toward the morgue where we had a friend of the family who helped pull miracles when it came to hiding bodies. Marty was a cousin from some distant uncle and he did magic with shooting victims. He was sought after all over Ireland for his embalming technique. If he didn't do this, I'd be worried about what he could do to people. Lucky, he was on our side.

I grabbed my phone from the console where I had left it and pulled up my brother Killian's number.

"Yeah?"

"I'm calling an emergency family meeting," I barked into the phone. "Meet me at the estate in half an hour."

"How serious is this?" he asked. It sounded like he was rolling out of bed.

"Just get your ass there and call Lorcan."

I hung up before he could respond, and I gunned it to the morgue. Pulling up at the back door, I dialed Marty.

"Marty," I started. "I'm outside. I need you to bring a gurney out and handle a body."

"Ah," he said, before his voice got a lot lower. "How many?"

"One. He's one of ours."

"Shit, I'll be there in a few minutes."

I got out of the car, and leaned against it, waiting for Marty to make his way out. No one had ever dared to do this to my father when he ran things. Maybe I needed to be as ruthless as he had been, bring this entire city to its knees.

Marty finally appeared with the gurney. The sound of the metal gurney vibrating from the gravel car park was loud in the quiet night air.

"Luke?" he said once he peered in the window. "How the hell?"

"Long story," I said. "Do it up right. He and his wife deserve that much."

Marty nodded. I helped him get Luke up on the gurney and I issued a quick prayer before Marty wheeled him away. I took a deep breath to calm myself down before I got back in the car and headed to the estate.

Our father's estate was one of the largest in the city, built by our great-great-grandfather over two centuries ago. My father had run his entire empire from the estate, but my brothers and I decided against it. It was used for parties, initiations and for family meetings.

I pulled up outside and noticed I was the first one here. Heading inside, I greeted Walter. He had served our father dutifully and now looked after the estate for us.

"Would you like me to cook you something for dinner, Conor?" he asked me.

"No," I said. "I won't be here for long. We just need a quick family meeting."

"All of you will be here?" he asked, surprised. "Please, let me bring you something."

"Fine, whatever is easy."

Walter headed off toward the kitchen and I headed into the dining room. Taking a seat, I waited, my anxiety hitting new peaks. Lorcan wouldn't be happy about this. He'd take it as a personal affront on him, as the oldest of all of us, he thought of himself as the toughest of us all.

Killian arrived with Lorcan in tow, both of them looked at me, and their smiles dropped.

They knew this was serious.

Walter put three glasses of whiskey down on the table and pretzels and nut mixes in small bowls between us.

"Speak," Lorcan said, gruffly.

"I lost a man tonight," I said. "We were meeting a seller, someone who obviously couldn't offload his guns unless it were to me, and he opened fire as we got out the car."

"Who the fuck was he?"

"Jye is looking into it now," I said. "He's a foreigner but if this gets out, it could mean serious shit."

"What do you need from us?" Killian asked.

"Backup when it's needed."

"You know you have that," Lorcan said. "If you can't handle the guns, we can take over, give you a hand."

I slammed my fist down on the table, the bowls jumped, spilling the contents over the table top. "I can handle it, but I need you to be there if I need it."

"Conor, united we can control Ireland just as da did, but if we're divided, it will cause issues. I'm just saying if you need help, you say it."

"Just keep an ear to the ground," I told him, annoyed.

"Got it," Killian said, acting the cool cat in between us as usual. "Let us know who we're looking out for when you have the information."

I nodded.

"Which guy did you lose?" Lorcan asked.

"Luke."

"Shit," Killian uttered under his breath, but it was loud enough for me to hear. "Did you tell Amity?"

"Jakob is doing it now."

"Make sure she doesn't get any stupid ideas," Lorcan said. "Grief can fuck up a lot of plans, brother."

"She hates me, that's why I sent Jakob."

"I'll go," Killian said. "I have a way with grieving widows."

Lorcan and I both rolled our eyes. Killian had always been a man whore, and he'd successfully swayed bereaved wives away from going to the cops for years.

"Go," I told him. "Amity is a hard ass, you'll have your work cut out for you."

"I've not met a pussy I haven't been able to tame," he said with a laugh as he headed out the door. I tossed back my whiskey, then Killian's. Lorcan wasn't sure I could handle my third of the business. He never thought I could, being the baby brother. But this was the first time anything has come up. Lorcan has had his fair share of shit go wrong but I had no problem bringing up, if I had to.

"I'm going back to the docks to find this fucker."

"Call me when you find him," he said. "I want to find out if this is going to affect our businesses as well."

I rolled my eyes as I headed out to my car. Speeding back to the docks, I tried not to scream out my frustration. As I waited at the street lights, I looked up to see the big cross in the sky. The church was a place I hadn't visited in a while, not since we lost our father.

Turning at the last minute to swerve into the carpark, I ran up the stairs and in through the large double doors. It was quiet inside, an altar of candles lit up the room, but the pews were almost in darkness. I sat down in the back, and bowed my head, sending a prayer to God. My religion had been a big part of who I was growing up, and it continued to be so. We had an agreement, me and God, that what I did was important and I only did it so Ireland could flourish.

Lately though, I'd been doubting my faith.

The door to the confessional opened and she emerged.

The girl from Peter Kennedy's shop.

His daughter.

She looked relieved. Which was the only response to a confessional you should have. She didn't see me sitting there, and I wondered why she was in confession so late at night.

As she left the church, I headed down to the confessional. Father Murphy was still sitting there.

"Father," I said.

"It's been a while," he replied. "What brings you back, my son?"

"I lost a man today," I told him. "He was shot in an ambush."

"His soul is with God now," Murphy said.

"The girl that was just in here," I said. "What do you know about her?"

"This is not what confessional is for, Conor."

"Just tell me, I'll find out one way or another. It's just easier if you tell me."

"Leave her be," he said, sternly. "She's been through enough. Now, light a candle for your lost man and spend time with God."

Father Murphy exited the confessional, leaving me wondering who the hell she was and why I couldn't stop thinking about her.

Fuck it.

Murphy was right. I got up and lit a candle for Luke and left the church.

TEEGHAN

WHY DID these bastard shopkeepers keep the cookies and chocolate bars at the checkout so I was standing next to it for minutes, contemplating how badly I needed to indulge. It had been a tough couple of days. Chocolate would solve my problems for all of five minutes and then I'd feel guilty about it on top of my problems.

I insisted on ignoring the problem sitting in their boxes, their metallic packaging calling me to them, beckoning for me to buy them.

Goddamn it. Why did they make the packaging so shiny?

"Next," I heard the cashier call out to me. She scanned my few items and bagged them as I searched in my bag for my card. Grabbing it out, I held it against the card reader until I heard the familiar beep. Picking up my bag, I headed out the sliding glass doors, just as I noticed who was standing in the carpark, talking to his friend.

Conor O'Farrell.

Perfect.

I headed to my car, hoping like hell he didn't notice me. Then again, he was after my father, not me. He wouldn't need to come speak to me.

As I approached my beaten up car, I pulled the boot up and put my groceries away. As I closed it and grabbed my keys out of my bag, I turned to see Conor standing there.

I gasped, shocked that I hadn't noticed him coming up to me, and stumbled back a bit.

"Jesus."

"Sorry," he said, with that undeniably cute smirk. "Didn't mean to startle ya."

I moved past him and tried to get in my car, but he ran in front of me again to stop me.

"It's nice to see you again."

"Have you fixed my father's door yet?"

I had no idea why I was being such a bitch to him. From what I'd been told, he was not one to mess with. His smirk was broad, but he didn't respond.

Before I did anything else stupid, I got in my car and waited for him to walk away before I took off at full speed to get back to my apartment.

I took my time getting out of my car and grabbing my groceries before I headed up the stairs. I pulled my keys out and tried to flip them around so I could get my house key free. I caught something out of the corner of my eye and turned to see Conor standing to the side of me. I gasped, my keys falling to the ground, and the bag slipping from my grasp. Conor reached out and grabbed the bag before everything tipped out.

"What are you doing here?" I asked, my heart still racing.

"Most people would say thank you," he said, that delicious smirk on his face again.

"Uh, thank you," I managed to get out.

"Are you going to head in, or did you want to hang out here in the hallway?"

I didn't want my neighbors to know I had for some reason registered on Conor's radar. Everyone would know who he was.

"Sure, come in," I said, leaning down and grabbing my keys to open the door. I looked around to see if I had left anything out, I shouldn't have. He walked in, put my grocery bag down on the counter to my kitchen and started to look around.

"Nice place," he said, turning back to look at me.

"Thank you."

He looked down at my dining table and picked up the letter I'd opened earlier. I made a move to grab it but stopped myself. It was no use.

"You know, I can take care of this for you."

I looked down at the divorce papers and sighed. "There's no use. It's done."

"Hopefully you got half of his shit," he said, putting the letter back down.

"I married a goddamn lawyer," I said. "Of course, I didn't."

"Like I said, I can fix it for you," he said.

"Why?" I countered. "Why do you care? You don't know me."

"No, I don't," he said. "And most of the time, I don't offer anything to anyone."

"Then why me?" I asked him.

He was wondering why himself when his phone began to ring. He pulled it from his pants but didn't say hello. Instead he held it to his ear and listened to whatever the hell the other person was saying.

"I'm coming."

He hung up and pocketed his phone again.

"I have to go," he said. Before I could respond, he was gone, and I was left reeling. What the hell was that?

I closed my door and locked it. My heart was still racing. Conor O'Farrell was in my apartment building. He knew where I lived, and obviously he had no qualms about visiting me whenever the hell he wanted.

Why the hell was he so goddamn sexy?

I could imagine that drop dead sexy smirk hovering over me as he slammed me into next week with what I imagined would be a very large and girthy dick.

He generated big dick energy.

I started to unpack my grocery bag, Conor very much still on my mind and a throbbing down below I didn't think I would experience after my horrific divorce.

CHAPTER THREE

TEEGHAN

I flipped through the big red book my mother had insisted on using for the books of this goddamn shop. It had taken me a good three weeks to figure out what was going on but my father refused to allow me to set him up online.

I was going to do it anyway and then show him that we can't do it in the book anymore. I looked back at last week's ledger but there was a payment that didn't make sense.

"Da?" I called out to him. He came from the back storeroom and headed toward me.

"Yeah?"

"What's this payment? It's not registered in your bills for the week."

He looked like I'd just caught him red handed. He had the nerve to look me in the eye and shrug.

"What is it, da?"

"It's nothing, just ignore it."

"I can't ignore it," I told him. "Is this what you pay the O'Farrell's?"

"No," he said. "It's a pledge for something else. Just mind your business, Teeghan."

"I can't do that. I'm running your books. I need to know, so tell me before I go to the bank."

"They won't tell you nothin'," he said. "It's done in cash so it doesn't matter."

"Then why did you put it in the business books?"

"Teeghan, just leave it."

"This is for Paul O'Brien, isn't it?" I stated, accusingly.

"You went from paying the goddamn Irish Mafia to paying for Paul to start a rebellion," I laid into him.

"You've been gone," he yelled at me. "You don't know how this place is run; it's always been this way. The O'Farrell's have run everything since their great granddaddy. I'm sick of paying for them to protect me from their own men."

"But now you're paying Paul," I said. "For what? You'd be better off with paying the O'Farrell's, at least then you won't get in trouble when Paul does you over because, believe me, he is using you."

"Leave it be, Teeghan," he said again. "I beg of you."

"I don't think Conor is so bad," I told him. "He could help you with Paul and his men. He can help you. I know for a fact you didn't pay Conor this much money every week."

He turned back around. "Don't you trust that snake of a man, Teeghan. He will eat you up and spit you back out again. Best you find yourself a new man, one who will keep his dick in his pants, marry and have children and leave this wretched town."

He left the shop front again, and I felt my anger mounting. Paul O'Brien and his goddamn lunatic sons needed to be stopped.

There was only one family in this town that could do anything about them.

CONOR

I pulled up outside my office at the docks. Jye stood with Jakob. Getting out of my car, I knew they had found the fucker responsible for killing Luke.

"Where was he?" I asked.

"Hiding out in Polkeen," Jye said. "He's a little rattled, but he should be able to form words."

I smirked at my oldest friend. "Where is he?"

"The dungeon."

I nodded and headed toward the storage container we had converted into a makeshift dungeon to hold our prisoners or to threaten those who dared to overshadow our business. It had one chair, a stinky bucket, chains from the ceiling and floor and one dingy light bulb so we could see what we were doing.

As I opened the door, the darkened container showed a tiny bit of light from outside to reveal a bloodied and dirty man, hanging from the chains attached to the ceiling. His hands were held high above his head, and he was struggling to stand up. He had one shoe on, one foot was bare. Jye sure did give him a workover before I got here. I flicked on the light of the container and closed the door behind me.

He looked up at me, wincing at the bright light, one eye was swollen shut, several cuts along his jaw and over the bridge of his nose.

"Do you know who I am?" I asked him, pulling the chair from the side of the room and sitting down on it.

He grunted but didn't speak.

"I will not ask again."

"Con-or O'Far-rell."

He was struggling to breathe, had a punctured lung or squashed esophagus.

"Good, now do you care to tell me why you shot at me and my men?"

His feet tried to shift the weight from one leg to another, but he slipped on the pool of blood under his feet. The chains clanged against each other, twisting with his weight, as he tried to get his balance again. The way he was leaning, it looked as if one of his shoulders had dislocated, the arm was at an unnatural angle above him.

He mumbled, blood spilling out of his mouth but I did hear him call me a pussy so I stood up and made my way toward him. He grimaced, fear taking any bravado he had left as he looked up at me.

"You came to my town, my country, and you tried to sell your guns without my direct permission," I said. "Then, you tried to take me out? Do you believe we would let you get away with it?"

"Kill me th-then," he blasted at me. Specks of blood splattered onto my shirt.

"Oh no," I said, as I looked him right in his good eye. "I wouldn't just simply kill you. No, that's too easy. I'd find your family, friends, anyone you love, and we'll end them, slowly torturing you knowing it was your fault, and you couldn't do a damn thing about it. Then we'd do you, but not until you're completely split from reality from your grief."

I could see he was scared but he didn't want me to see it.

"I don't love anybody," he spat at my face. I used my sleeve to wipe off the mix of saliva and blood from my face.

"Yes you do," I said, getting really close to his face.

"Your eyes told me you did and believe me, we'll find them, we'll find all of them."

"What do you want?" he asked me.

"I want to know why you came here," I said. "Who sent you to us?"

"You stopped me from selling, I had to come to you."

"No," I stopped him before he dug himself deeper. "Someone told you to come to Ireland."

"We had an opportunity," he replied slowly. "No one was buying in Asia."

"I don't believe you," I said in his ear as I circled him. He stiffened when I did so. Acting as if I were the shark to his school of fish. It was a tactic my father had taught me, and it had never failed.

Jye had left a steel pipe in the dungeon, how convenient. I walked over to it and ran the edge of it along the storage walls. It made an awkward squealing sound that the man cried out at. As I made my way back to him, I waited for him to speak, to tell me who his contact was. Who the hell was the one trying to come after my business?

No one had dared touch an O'Farrell in decades, I couldn't let it be me where that fear ends. I'd never hear the end of it from Lorcan.

"Speak."

He looked me in the eye, a silent fuck you, and spat at me again.

This motherfucker.

"So be it," I replied, pulling the steel pipe back and slamming it into his side. He groaned and winced as he tried to right his stance yet again. His legs were getting tired, and his body was slumping, pulling on his chains from the ceiling. I continued to hit him with the pipe in the side of the abdomen, then the other side. The pipe was hitting his skin at odd angles, ripping it open. Blood splattered all over his chest and the floor. He couldn't lift his head anymore, but I could hear him groaning. I moved to the side of the container, taking in deep breaths as I dropped the steel pipe with a clank on the ground.

I pressed the button for the chains hanging from the ceiling to release. He fell so quickly, he couldn't pull his hands in place to stop his face from hitting the cement floor. I heard a sickening crunch when he fell, and his rapid breathing told me I broke something.

I made my way back over to him, kicking him with my foot to turn over onto his back. He looked up at me, his one good eye, bloodied and searching for an end to the torture.

"Last chance, bud."

The gurgling that was coming from him being on his back made me realize he wouldn't be able to talk anyway.

Shit.

I kicked his head hard, it jerked to the side, with a popping sound. I'd always been good at breaking necks with a swift kick but this guy had just made it so easy.

The rapid breathing, gurgling and splattering was gone. Instead, he laid there, limp, his one eye opened in and bloody.

I sighed before I headed back out of the storage container and wiped my hands on my shirt. Jye and Jakob waited for me.

"Clean that piece of shit up," I said. "Drop him in the bay and find out how I can get someone else who knows the fuck is up with his enterprise."

Jye nodded and I headed back to my office to clean off. I had been within a hand grasp of the truth of who was trying to kill our empire, but it was just out of reach.

It was infuriating.

CHAPTER FOUR

TEEGHAN

"Another?" I asked my sister-in-law Sloane as I tossed the last of my drink back. She nodded and I headed up to the bar to order another round. The bartender, Logan, nodded at me to signal that he knew we needed another round and went to work pouring the drinks for us. Within minutes, our two cocktails were sitting on the counter. I swiped my card on the reader and headed back to the table. I'd only come to this club a few times since I had been back, but Logan already knew me and my drink order.

I didn't know whether to be flattered or horrified.

Sloane took the cocktail from me and started sipping away at the concoction that tasted like bubblegum and cotton candy.

"Sweet Jesus," she said, giggling. "These drinks are positively divine."

"Keep an eye on the number you drink, they may taste like lollies, but they are potent as all hell," I told her with a chuckle. It had been great seeing Sloane again, since getting married to an Englishman, I had hardly come back to Ireland. Sloane had been so disappointed in my choice of husband that she almost hadn't come to the wedding.

"He's cute," she said, pointing to the blonde Adonis on the dance floor. He had been the only one I noticed dancing all night. He was about a foot taller than everyone else, and had a new dance partner every song. The lineup of girls, biting their lower lip and dancing half-heartedly off to the side told me he was the only piece of meat they wanted in this club. He wasn't my type, though. I liked the darker features, the ones where you could tell their eyes were as dark as their souls. Another reason why marrying the blond Englishman had been a terrible idea.

Really, what had I been thinking?

I looked up at the balcony above, where I knew the O'Farrell's conducted business. To my surprise, they were all there. Three brothers, one empire that controlled all of Ireland.

Conor was relaxing into his chair, a black collared shirt on, rolled up to his elbows to reveal the tail end of a tattoo on his left arm, mid forearm. I found myself wondering what he had tattooed on him. The first couple of buttons were undone, revealing yet another tattoo on his chest. His hair, usually slicked back, was now falling to the side, reminding me a little of a young Elvis Presley.

Sloane shook my hand, snapping my attention back to her. I was met with a worried expression.

"What are you doing?" she asked me. "You know how dangerous they are, don't let them catch you staring."

I rolled my eyes. "They wouldn't notice anyone down here."

"Oh please, you know, Killian leaves here with a new woman every night."

Her tone was tense and a little off, like she was jealous or bitter. That's when I remembered. "Wait, wasn't Killian your high school boyfriend?"

Sloane had been three years above me in school, but I always remembered her. She'd been such a beautiful soul in school, always helping everyone, stopping bullies from picking on the poor and the fat. But I did remember her always having a boyfriend, and that was Killian. I was sure of it. I hadn't gone to school with Conor, and I wondered why that was.

"Drop it," she said. "I'd rather not remember back to those days. It's bad enough I'm this close to him."

I chuckled, seeing her mild discomfort. When she'd married my brother Sean, I could never understand how someone like my brother could land a stone-cold fox-like Sloane but it all came down to her heart. She'd loved how goofy he was, and that he was always making her laugh.

That was until he died a few years ago. She hadn't been able to meet anyone new since, and frankly, it didn't look like she wanted to.

"So you can't exactly lecture me on who to stare at now, can ya?"

She rolled her eyes this time. "That was a teenage Killian, not the monster you see now."

"I don't think Conor is so bad," I told her. "Every time I've run into him, he's been helpful and sweet."

Sloane's eyes got bigger. "Every time? There's been more than one time?"

"Well, yes, and admittedly the first time I saw him, he wasn't doing something great but since then, he's just popped up at places I've been and he's been charming even when I've been rude to him."

"And he's been nice to you?" she asked. I could tell she

didn't believe me.

"Yes."

"Oh, Tee. You're on his radar, that's not a good place to be."

I shrugged my shoulders. "It's not like it'll be a long lasting impression. I leave in a few weeks, remember?"

She nodded but there was a faraway look in her eyes. She was thinking about something deep. Silence descended on us and I kept an eye on the dance floor for any willing participants in some hanky panky.

I doubted I would pick someone. It had been way too long between sex bouts for me to even think about it right now. Yet, even though I hadn't engaged in the act, I still went to my wax appointments and stripped any hair down there from my body.

Just in case.

"It's getting late," she said. "I'm going to the bathroom."

"I'll get us one more drink," I told her. She sighed but nodded and walked off to the bathroom. Heading over to the bar, I motioned for Logan with two fingers. He nodded and set to work. I rested one elbow on the bar and kept an eye out for Sloane.

As I scoured the dancefloor, I saw someone come up to me at the bar. Turning my head back, I gasped when I saw Conor standing in front of me, that little smirk on his lips. He smelt so goddamn good.

"Hello again," he said.

"Hi."

"I didn't know you came here," he said. "I would have noticed you."

"Well maybe you aren't here on the same nights as me," I told him, ignoring the fact that my brain was swooning already.

"Maybe that's it," he replied with a smile. Logan put the drinks down in front of me and for some reason I wished I had been drinking my normal bourbon instead of these girly drinks. "Are you here with anyone?"

"My sister-in-law."

"Oh," he said, looking around. "Abandoned you, has she?"

"No, but she probably wouldn't be too happy with you and I talking right now."

He chuckled, a deep and masculine laugh that had the nerves in my crotch sparking to life.

"Why is that?"

"Because of who you are, I suppose. You do have a bit of a reputation."

"A bit?" he repeated. "Well, that's the nicest way anyone has ever said it."

"I aim to please," I replied, finding this conversation mildly erotic for some weird reason. I should be running away but I wanted to be here. I wanted to be in front of his gorgeous face, those eyes that were penetrating.

"I wanted to tell you I had your father's shop door fixed," he told me. "Even though it was smashed for good reason."

"Well, maybe it was, but my father is a tight ass, he wouldn't pay for a new one himself."

"Sounds stubborn, perhaps that's where you get it from?"

Stubborn is one of the nicest ways I've been described. I thought of the transaction in my father's books that I had discovered earlier.

"I thought you should know, if you're after who is funding the rebellion, you may want to look at Paul O'Brien. My da had been paying him rather than you and from what I was able to gather, it's much bigger than a simple rebellion. He's got it out for you and your whole damn family."

His smirk dropped and his eyes became stony. I was instantly intimidated, and a little horny. Had I done the wrong thing by talking shop with him?

"Thank you," he said. "I had half put it to him, but you just clarified it. It appears I'm in your debt."

Oh, good lord.

"We'll call it even with the door," I said, noticing my voice was a little uneven. He'd shaken me to the core with one line.

That devilish smirk was back. What was it about this man that I couldn't ignore?

"Your sister in law is probably right," he told me, the smirk fading and a troubled expression taking over. "You should stay away from me."

"I'm not the one who keeps appearing wherever I am," I replied. "That's on you, buddy."

That smirk was back again. Oh god, I would do anything for that man when he smirked at me like that. As he was about to say something else, I heard a loud bang. Everyone ducked down, and turned around to see what the source of the noise was. Conor pulled me from the chair and had me duck down. He pushed me toward the end of the bar and had me take cover on the other side.

"Stay here," he ordered. "I'll tell you when to come out."

I felt my heart in my throat, my breathing was incredibly labored, to the point I thought I would pass out. Gunfire could be heard somewhere over the bar, lights were going out, screams echoed in the club, the glass behind the bar was bursting, the liquid spilling everywhere. Logan had taken off, god knows where, and it was just me behind here.

I saw in one of the mirrors that littered the dancefloor that there were two shooters, and the O'Farrell's were facing off with them, guns drawn.

My phone pinged. I quickly wrestled it out of my pocket and looked down at the message from Sloane.

"Did you get out?"

I keyed in my passcode and replied, "No. I'm hidden behind the bar. No one can see me."

"OMG. I'm calling the cops."

Quickly, I replied. "No. Just wait. It looks like the shooters are out of ammo."

I knew she would already be on the phone to the cops, but I didn't want them to burst in. Surely Conor would be blamed, and probably have to pay out an arm and a leg just to get out of jail.

God, Tee, why do you even care about them?

But I did. I had no idea why, but I didn't want Conor to suffer.

Finally, the shooting stopped and now all I heard was yelling. My heart felt as if it would burst from my chest, I was anxious, like I'd never experienced before.

Suddenly, I gasped when I saw Conor lean down from above the bar.

"Come on."

I let him take my hand in his, leading me down the back, past the bathrooms and to the fire safety door.

"You can leave through here," he said. He opened the door for me and I stepped through, walking away, shooting him one last look before he closed the door. I headed down the alley and toward the main road where I saw only Sloane standing, her phone in her hand, and a very worried look on her face.

"You didn't call the cops?" I queried, surprised.

"You told me not to."

"I didn't think you would actually listen."

"Well, this is the O'Farrell's club, they wouldn't turn up anyway," she mused, slinging her arm through mine as we headed toward her apartment complex just a few blocks away. "That's another good reason to steer clear of them. They own the coppers."

She was right. Tonight should have told me enough to scare me away. Three weeks and I'll be gone, I needed to keep my head on right and steer clear of Conor O'Farrell.

CONOR

"Who the fuck was that?" Lorcan rounded on me as I made my way back to my brothers. Killian had beat the crap out of the shooters and they were now knocked out in front of us, on chairs.

"Nobody."

"Didn't look like a nobody," he said. "Actually, looked like she had quite the body."

"Shut the fuck up," I found myself getting angry at him. "She just got caught up in the club at a bad time."

Killian was suss too but he didn't say anything. He never did, but he would side with Lorcan anyway, even if he was on my side of the fence.

"Why don't we focus on this shit?" I pointed at the two idiots. "How is it that we are getting shot at, two out of three businesses now attacked. They're losing their fear in us."

"This started with you," Killian said. "Why the hell haven't you sorted that shit out yet?"

"I have," I spat at him. "Problem is someone in Ireland, probably Galway, is inviting these cocksuckers in."

"Who?" Lorcan asked me.

"I'll bet all my money on Paul O'Brien."

"Paul?" Killian repeated. "He's a bitter old man, not capable of setting this up."

"No, but he has two sons who have both been to university. I'm betting on their help to get a little rebellion going."

"Well, we need to deal with them," Lorcan offered.

"No shit, sherlock."

"Well, how do you suppose we do that?"

"I have it on good authority that he's the head of the rebellion, enlisting shop owners on the bay to support him. They've been pledging their protection money to this fucking rebellion."

"We need to bring him and those bastard sons of his in," Killian said. "They're fuckin' imbeciles anyway. I went to school with them, they may have gone to university, but I highly doubt they could pull this off on their own."

"I'll have Jye round them up," I said, pulling my phone free and dialing.

Killian went back to the men and searched everywhere for some kind of ID. Lorcan was pouring himself a shot at the bar.

I told Jye where to find the O'Brien's and went to the bar for my own drink. It was needed tonight.

"I thought you would never settle down, little brother," he said to me, tossing his shot back quickly.

"I don't know what you're talking about," I replied, hoping like hell to avoid this conversation.

"You wouldn't just protect anyone like that, Conor," he said, turning to me now as he poured himself another one. "I have watched you grow up. You've never cared about anyone but yourself."

"Honestly, Lor, drop this fucking shit. I helped someone

34

out of the club so we could conduct business. If I truly wanted to keep this from you, I would have left her there, wouldn't I?"

"You know that once you bring someone in, they're the one you marry, no one else can know how we operate or how far of a reach we have."

"I know, Lorcan, I was raised with our father as well."

It was one of the reasons I didn't think of women as anything but a piece of ass. I didn't want to settle down to one woman, how fucking boring was that?

Images of Tee on my bed, some sexy lingerie on, as she looked up at me, biting the bottom of her lip flitted through my mind. I closed my eyes and tossed back my drink, letting the burn of the whiskey settle in. Anything to get the sexy images out of my head.

I'd never liked red heads before, but with those bewitching green eyes and those red Merida curls, I was a goner.

How the hell had she turned my dick into a ride at Disneyland, going up and down, up and down around her like a goddamn see saw.

"Just keep an eye on her," he said, finishing off the bottle. "I know a Kennedy when I see one, their family have always had it out for ours. Don't let me remind you what Peter Kennedy's father did to our grandfather."

How could I forget? It had only been told to me several times a year, especially when the uncles and father would get stuck into their cigars and whiskey.

Lorcan walked off to join Killian. I decided to wait for word from Jye before I joined them again. I had every faith in Jye's ability to track down the O'Briens.

I still couldn't get my dick to calm the fuck down and I was half drunk from the whiskey I had been throwing back.

Half drunk and I couldn't lose my boner, what the fuck was going on? Surely she was a witch, only a witch could make me lose control like this. I headed down the hall to the men's bathroom and locked myself in the disabled cubicle. It was the only one that had four walls down to the floor to hide someone in here. I turned the door handle and locked it behind me, pulling my jeans down past my ass and whipping my hard cock out. I spat in my hand and grabbed a hold of my cock, closing my eyes and putting one hand against the cool tiles on the wall for leverage. Starting with smooth, delicate rubs, I began to slowly pump my cock, thinking of her sweet mouth wrapped around the head of my cock. My balls began to ache with need as I gripped my cock tight, squeezing it for all it was worth. I imagined those bright green eyes which reminded me of emeralds, looking up at me, as her mouth was stretched over the girth of my cock. I felt the nerves in my cock spark to life as I ground out a strangled moan as my cum spurt all over the side of the wall. I moved so I could lean against the other wall to get my breath back. Goddamn it.

I'd never cum so quickly doing it myself before.

It was her.

It was that goddamn witch.

She had my head in all sorts of panic, grief, whatever the fuck it was, I didn't know because I had never experienced it before.

I didn't even know the fucking woman and she had me at odds with myself. I couldn't do this. I couldn't be getting like this around her, because it could mean the difference between being a successful O'Farrell, and death.

I cleaned myself up and went back to face the music. My phone dinged and I checked the message as I got back to my brothers.

Jye had found the O'Brien's and they were in his car, coming here.

TEEGHAN

I COULDN'T STOP THINKING about tonight. I'd left Sloane's apartment an hour ago, even though she had protested that I shouldn't be alone tonight, I had been pacing my own apartment ever since. Every little sound made me jump, and fried my nerves. I tossed back a shot of whiskey to calm myself. The sound of someone knocking on my door had me jumping so high, I almost actually had my feet leaving the ground. I cautiously made my way to the door, took a deep breath and opened it quickly.

I was confronted with Conor O'Farrell.

He looked angry. Homicidal angry and yet, I didn't feel fear. I felt...fuck...was I turned on?

Yep, that was the tingly sensation I felt down south. In this moment, I didn't even care if he had come here to kill me, as long as he fucked me first.

He stopped leaning against my door, and he took one step inside, I launched myself into his arms, our mouths meeting hard. I could feel how hard his lips were against mine as he devoured my mouth with his. He picked me up, wrapping my legs around his waist without disconnecting our mouths and walked me back into the apartment, kicking the door shut with the back of his heel.

I felt the heat coming from between us, radiating off him with ferocity. I pulled at his shirt, undoing the buttons quickly and gliding the material down his arms. We parted our lips for a moment as I ran my nails down his hairless chest, feeling every ripple, every dip along his tight body.

"We shouldn't do this," he said, putting me back down. I landed on my feet hard as he stepped back, his shirt still open, baring that glorious tatted chest of his. "I'm not the kind of guy you need."

I didn't want to think, I wanted him, all of him, I could regret it in the morning. For now, I needed release, and the only kind of release I needed, he was going to give to me.

"Oh shut up," I said, exasperated. I closed the distance between us, my hand reaching up to grab his neck and force him down to kiss me. He grabbed me by the hips and shoved me against the wall, his leg in between my legs, holding me in place as he pulled my shirt over my head, my bra was gone in seconds. He looked down at my bare breasts and I could have sworn he growled.

Growled.

Like a fucking lion.

He pushed me down the hall, with me walking backward until I got to the bedroom. He shoved me down on the bed. I looked up at him, the predator within very evident. I could see how people would think he was scary. He had that thing in his eye, the one you see in killers. He pulled his shirt off his arms, throwing it to the side of the room. Next, he undid his belt, and zip, and slowly rolled his jeans over his tight hips.

Oh Lord, I thought, as I took in his hard cock caught underneath his boxers. He was huge judging by the size of the lump.

"Take off your jeans," he said to me, his voice full of desire. I undid the button and zip, swiveling my hips as I laid on the bed to get them down past my ass. He helped me once I got them over my hips, by ripping them down my legs, freeing me. His eyes glazed over once again as he took in my matching purple lace panties that matched the bra, he all but ripped off me moments ago. I felt a little self-conscious about my tummy on display. I used to be taut and toned, but since the divorce I really didn't know how to care about my strict eating and exercise regimen.

He pulled his boxers down, freeing that bobbing cock in all its glory. I couldn't take my eyes off it.

"You like what you see?"

I nodded my head without taking my eyes off the head of that glorious piece of manhood.

He knelt on the bed, next to me, the cock jutting out over my face. I maneuvered myself so I could take my hand and wrap it around his cock. He was thick as fuck, and for a moment I was scared of how he'd get inside of me. How cliche, right? Hottest of hot guys, and he's thick as a tree stump down there.

Slowly, I licked a path around the head of his cock, before I took him into my mouth. He groaned as I slowly pulled him free of my mouth.

"Damn it, woman."

I liked having this power over him. He braced himself against the wall with his hands as I feasted on his cock. I grabbed the base of his cock and squeezed as I ticked the head of it with my tongue. The look on his face told me he was losing control and quickly.

"Fuck," he called out, pounding his fist into the wall. Thankfully it didn't break. In one fluid motion, he swept me off his cock and underneath him. He yanked at my panties so hard they ripped into pieces as he shifted my legs over his shoulders and pulled my ass off the bed. My shoulders were bearing the brunt of my weight as I felt his mouth dive down onto my pussy. I fisted the sheets around me, the corners threatening to give way as his tongue plundered my soft flesh. His moans as he dug his tongue around my clit had my pussy throbbing already.

I screamed out as one of his fingers delved into me, moving in rhythm with his tongue. My eyes were rolling into the back of my head as the pleasure assaulted my senses. I felt my hips begin to gyrate as my pussy began to throb heavily. My orgasm hit me harder than I expected it would and I screamed out his name as my pussy walls spasmed and my hips rolled out the waves of ecstasy.

I didn't have time to recover before I felt him shift my legs down off his shoulders and around his waist. My eyes opened just as his cock slammed into me. He groaned as he felt my walls clench around him, adjusting to his girth.

"Fuck," he grunted as he pulled himself out and slowly, drove himself into me again. His fingers ground into my hips as he picked up his pace, slamming his cock all the way into me, lifting my ass up so he could get deeper. I'd never been in such nirvana before. My pussy was clenching around him, trying to grip onto him and never let go. He filled me with such intensity that I didn't want him to ever pull out either.

But this was Conor fucking O'Farrell, there was no way he would ever want another fuck from me. This was it.

So I better fucking enjoy it.

I pushed him onto his back, somehow he allowed me to take the reins. I slid back down on his cock, my hips moving back and forth as I rode him. He looked up at me, those wild eyes boring a hole into my very soul. I couldn't tell what he was thinking right now. I should be scared. I should be running for the hills, but I couldn't seem to part from him. I needed him, I needed his cock inside of me and I needed for him to scream out my name.

I pushed my hands down on his pecs, over the tattoo of

Celtic knots that spread over both his pecs and looked down at the crest on his breastplate. That tattoo had to have hurt, it was right over bone. This motherfucker was hard as nails and right now, his cock was doing things to my insides that none other had. I moved my hips in a circle, his cock going with me. His eyes widened, his mouth carving into an O as the sensations that were running through me, surely were running down his cock too. His fingers dug into my hips again but it didn't stop me. I welcomed the pain.

I wanted him to mark me.

I wanted a way to remember this because it would never be topped again. I knew it. I was scared of him, and yet, oddly not scared enough. I knew he could do real damage to me if he wanted to. He could make me disappear if he wanted to and frankly that excited me to no end.

I felt his cock harden even more inside of me, his breathing was becoming labored as I picked up my pace, bobbing up and down on him.

Conor launched me onto my back, holding one leg up, he slammed into me hard. I clutched at the blankets around me to hold onto as he pummeled into me, time and time again. Sweat beaded on his forehead as he continued to assault my pussy.

Conor pulled out of me, and in one movement, he flipped me onto my stomach. I didn't have time to right myself before he pulled my ass up into the air and kicked my ankles apart. Slowly, he positioned his cock back at my pussy and slammed into me from behind. I gasped at the sheer pleasure shooting up from my pussy. I pushed up on my hands so I was kneeling. Conor grabbed my neck with one hand, and squeezed slightly, as he took my earlobe between his teeth. My pussy pulsed with excitement as he slammed into me. His teeth grazing my ear with every slam.

His hand tightened on my throat so it made it hard to breathe but in this moment of pure bliss I didn't care if I was breathing or not. He let go of my ear, but his hand remained as he continued to slam into me. One hand on my throat, another on my hip. I felt like I was in heaven.

His grip on my hip got harder and his hand left my throat, to take my other hip as he felt my pussy tighten, the waves returning for round two as I exploded around his cock, clenching him hard. He rode out my orgasm but once I started to moan from the intensity, he called *Teeghan* and shot into me over and over again.

CONOR

I LOOKED over at the angel with the wild hair laying on the opposite end of the bed. Her eyes were glazed and she had a smirk on her face. I'd never wanted a woman more in my life and I knew right here and now, this wouldn't be the last time I invaded her pussy.

"What?" she asked me.

"I'm just lookin'."

"I'm aware."

I smirked at her, knowing I was making her feel uneasy. I liked doing that, but I hated it when she tried to cover up. I yanked at the quilt between us so she couldn't cover that beautiful body. It wasn't like the skinny girls that usually tried to mount me, she had a real body, with real curves. I'd loved feeling the skin in between my fingers as I gripped onto her hips. The memory alone was making my cock twitch.

"Who is Merida?" she asked me suddenly.

"Why?"

"You called out the name Merida. I wanted to be mad, but I was amidst an orgasm that was about to level me."

"No, I remember calling your actual name."

"The first go round, sure, but the second time," she said with a smile. "You called out Merida."

"You remind me of a Disney character with your crazy hair."

She twisted her finger in one of her curls and smiled. "The redhead from *Brave*?"

I nodded. "In my head, you're Merida so I guess it slipped out."

"A big tough mafia guy watching cartoons?" she replied. "Not at all what I expected."

"And what did you expect?"

She was silent for a moment, judging whether or not she should speak her mind. I desperately wanted her to. I wanted to know what was on that gorgeous mind of hers.

"A shootout at the club, followed by red hot sex."

I felt the chuckle before I heard it and she smiled at my response. God that smile could melt me. I'd never felt like that with anyone before.

She had to be a witch, right?

"What's on your chest?" she asked me, looking down at my tattoo. I looked down and sighed. Not many women asked me about my tattoos, probably because I never really stuck around after but I was enjoying this time just sitting on the bed.

"It's my family crest," I told her. "Surrounded by a shit ton of shamrocks and Celtic knots."

"Must have taken a while," she said. "It's pretty detailed."

"Do you have any?" I asked her.

She nodded. "Yeah, I have one on my ankle."

I looked down and saw the outline of a flower. "Cute."

"Thanks."

I felt like there was something more behind the tattoo though and desperately I found I wanted to know what it was for. "Why the lily?"

"It's my favorite flower. Actually, it's in memory of my brother. He died a few years ago."

"I'm sorry," I said, honestly. As much as my brothers drove me crazy, I wouldn't like to know what it would be like to lose one of them. "He liked them too?"

"No," she chuckled. "He always got me one for my birthday. See, my parents were always hungover or drunk on my birthday, so they never really remembered to do anything for it. My brother always got me a lily from some neighboring house for my birthday until he got a job, then he bought me a bouquet for my birthday after that."

"That's nice. I can't imagine Peter being drunk and hungover much though."

"He's not," she told me. "I'm born the day after St Patrick's day."

"Tough break there," I laughed. She smiled along with me. It was odd to feel this at ease with a near stranger. A near stranger I had just fucked the brains out of, nonetheless. Her eyes were getting droopy which meant she would fall asleep soon. I had to fight off the drowsiness myself because I never slept in a strange bed, and I never stayed the night.

But this bed was getting comfortable and I was finding it hard to get the will to leave.

What the fuck was happening to me?

CHAPTER FIVE

CONOR

The unfamiliar sounds of the morning woke me up. I looked around me to find an unfamiliar bedroom. My own apartment was sound proofed, so I never heard the birds in the morning. I turned to look down at the mop of red hair on the pillow next to me.

Teeghan Kennedy.

Last night had been exactly what I needed to get her off my mind. She'd been up for anything, and her stamina had rivaled mine.

Now *that* had never happened before.

I got up, without disturbing her, and grabbed my clothes from the floor. Her lingerie lay in tatters on the floor. I made a mental note to buy her new ones. My animalistic side took over last night, but I didn't regret it, and I sure as shit knew she wouldn't either.

But it was done.

Now I could go on without thinking about her again.

Right?

I left the apartment as quickly as I could and jogged down the stairs to my car outside. I'd left my phone in my car and could now see everyone had been looking for me last night.

I dialed Jye first as I peeled out of the street Teeghan lived on.

"Meet at the estate," Jye said. "Your brothers called us in for a meeting first thing."

Oh great. The one time I don't use my phone, World War 3 starts. I shot out a quick text to my brothers saying I was on my way as I checked the clock on my car radio.

Shit. Since when have I slept past nine in my life?

It was going to be fun explaining this one away. Ah fuck it, they didn't need to know it was with Teeghan, they could assume I'd found someone to fuck into the night, to release all the pressure in my groin.

As I turned into the estate, I put my game face on. I'd never felt so relaxed after last night. Usually, I wouldn't fall asleep in the bed either. I took off right after, but after our sexathon last night and into the early morning hours, there was no way I could drive when I had been so heavily drained.

Parking next to Jye's car, I headed inside. They were all seated at the family table. The O'Brien boys were tied to chairs at the end. I swatted Jeremiah on the back of the head as I walked past. I hated that motherfucker.

"Thank you for joining us," Killian sneered toward me.

"You're welcome."

My carefree response only ignited his anger further. Lorcan stood up, putting his hands up to either of us to silence us just like our dad used to.

"Now, we brought you here to talk," he aimed at Jeremiah and Ronan O'Brien. "We know you are the brains behind the rebellion. Let's talk terms."

"Terms?" Ronan spat. "We don't recognize you as the authority in this area."

"The O'Farrell's have always been in charge," he said, gritting his teeth. "Since we founded this town."

"Founded?" Jeremiah laughed. "We all know the Kennedy's founded this goddamn town."

"Get your facts straight," Killian shot back at them.

"Why the fuck are we talking about history?" I started. "Can we get back to why we're here?"

Jeremiah shot a fuck you look toward me which made me laugh. He and I had had our history, mostly, I'd fucked every single woman who had dared to bed him. The last one he'd been engaged to, but it went further than that. It went back to school when he had gotten close to the girl I liked back then, back before I was who I am today. Maybe it shaped me into who I was, maybe not, who the fuck knew. All I knew for sure was I hated Jeremiah fucking O'Brien.

"Look," I said. "You get in our way again or you hire people to shoot up our places of business, and we'll come for you, and any one you care about. Your daddy ain't going to be around to save you every single time."

"You leave him alone," Ronan tried to act intimidating in his chair but he couldn't move properly. "Your beef is with us."

"Well rumor has it, your old man is the one who is preventing the other shop owners from paying us."

"And just to tell ya, I have no problem taking out your entire rebellion, one at a time."

Jeremiah's eyes were intense, just the right amount of anger behind them. I think they understood. They knew we had every resource at our fingertips. We'd been on top for generations for a good reason.

"Gentlemen, we can be here for as long as you need."

Lorcan's domineering voice bellowed over everyone muttering to themselves. Everyone fell silent and we all looked up at him. He looked so much like our father these days.

"Now, start talking," he said, sitting down in his chair. Ronan looked to Jeremiah, who I knew would be the first to break.

It was only a matter of time.

TEEGHAN

"What's up with you?" Sloane asked. "You seem way too happy for someone who was almost killed by a madman last night."

I rolled my eyes at her and stuffed the last of my toast in my mouth to stop myself from speaking and betraying my true feelings. Last night had been the best sex of my entire life and I highly doubted I would ever experience it again.

But it's what I needed.

A thorough pounding, now I could stop imagining what Conor looked like naked. He had a large tattoo on his chest that connected up to his shoulders and down to a large tattoo on his back. I'd seen it when he had been leaving, believing me to be asleep. It was even more detailed on the back than on his front. A large Celtic cross went from his shoulders down to his waist, two flaming swords on either side of the cross.

"OK, spill it."

"Spill what?" I asked.

"What did you do after you went home?" she asked me, annoyed.

"I had sex," I told her.

"With whom?" Sloane asked. "That single dad neighbor of yours on the fifth floor?"

I hated that she still remembered that. I'd mentioned it once when I had been drunk, and no, I still didn't know his name because I hadn't spoken to him since I found out he lived in my building. As per usual, I had embarrassed myself in front of him.

"No."

"Well, who else do you know in town?" she asked me, sitting back in her chair and watching me like a hawk.

"Can't you just be happy that I finally got laid?"

Sloane looked at me without speaking before leaning forward. "Don't tell me you called Conor?"

"I did not call him," I told her, trying to be as vague as possible.

"Shit, Tee. This isn't good. You would do yourself good to leave for London as soon as possible before he stops you from leaving ever again."

I rolled my eyes. "It was one night of unbridled passion, he's probably already moved on to some other strumpet."

Sloane shook her head. "I'm worried about you."

"Why do you hate him so much when you don't know him?"

"*You* don't know him, Teeghan," she said. "Please, god, please don't see him again. Just leave before you get stuck here again."

She was pleading with me with so much passion, it made me wonder why she hated the O'Farrell's so badly. She also never used my full name. I was always Tee to her, even in school when she took pity on the junior who had no friends.

She knew the O'Farrell's so I should listen to her advice but there was something about Conor, something that, yes, was a little scary, but I also knew he was someone I could trust with my life. I didn't know how that was even possible but it's what I felt.

"What happened with you and Killian?" I asked her.

She sighed, and sat back in her chair, avoiding my eyes. "That's past history."

"Obviously if you hate them so much, it's not."

She finally looked back at me. "Well, it is. I married your brother, remember. I loved your brother more than anything."

I saw the pain in her eyes but I couldn't help but wonder if the pain also encompassed whatever happened with Killian as well my brother's untimely death. We rarely spoke about him, because I knew it still pained her that they'd only been wed for a short amount of time, thinking they had the rest of their lives for children and such, and in an instant he was gone.

Sean and I were close, but we did butt heads from time to time as all siblings did. He never forgave me for moving away and marrying an Englishman. That was when our relationship became strained and he always blamed me for breaking ma's heart. It hurt beyond belief when I lost him, especially since we'd never patched things up. When ma had died just a year ago, it had hit dad even more. He hadn't been coping at all but still, I didn't come back until my marriage imploded.

I still felt guilty over that to this day.

"I know you did," I said. "No one is doubting that, Sloane."

"Let's just drop it," she said, finishing her coffee and putting her napkin on her plate. "I've given you the warning on him, and I'm done with it. If you choose to play with your life by continuing to have fanciful ideas with him, then that is on you."

She grabbed her bag and headed inside to pay for our breakfast. I sighed and finished my coffee and waited for her to come back out.

Killian really must have done a number on her and I was desperate to find out what happened.

CHAPTER SIX

CONOR

The lights were still on in the shop but I knew Peter never kept his shop open this late. I wondered if I was going to walk in on a secret meeting. I opened the door to the shop, it was still unlocked. Stepping inside, the bell above the door jangled, announcing my arrival.

Peter came from the back of the shop, confused, before his expression quickly switched to fear.

"Conor," he said. "I've been meaning to thank you for the door. It was not necessary."

"You can thank your precocious daughter for that, she was really quite insistent."

"I am sorry if she bothered you, I'll have a word with her."

"It's not necessary," I told him. "In fact, I have come for information on something else."

Peter nodded.

"This rebellion, who is behind it?"

"I have re-pledged my protection money to you, Conor,

I will not be associated with a rebellion. Truth be, I lost everything in recent years. I've lost a wife, a son, and my family's house. The very house I hoped to pass down to my only living child but the economy has not been fair to an old man like me. I will not be an enemy, Conor, to you or your brothers."

"I appreciate it, Peter, I do, but I didn't come here to hassle you. I came here for information. I happen to know Paul O'Brien has been a bad influence on you, but I don't hold that against you. We've all been influenced incorrectly in the past. I just need to know how many we're dealing with."

"To be honest, I wasn't that involved in it. I know of the O'Brien's and the Kelly's."

"Surely, it's more than that."

"No doubt about it," he told me. "Paul knew I did not want to be a leader of it, I merely helped with funding and mostly out of loyalty to our family's long held friendship."

"When did it start?"

"A few months back for me," he said. "But I'm sure it has been brewing for years. As you know, when your father passed, a lot of the older shop owners thought we could have our money back."

"We are protecting you," I said, leaning against a counter. "You do realize that, don't you?"

"The only damage I've ever had was you smashing through my door," he replied.

"Because we protect you, and your interests," I cut back at him. "If anyone were to hurt you or your business, or even your family, we would come for them with a fiery vengeance."

"Anyway, I don't have any more information to give you," he said, changing the topic. It was probably for the best, I didn't want to lose my mind here again. Doors weren't so cheap.

"You will not see any rebuttal from this," I said. "If you are threatened or feel that you are no longer safe, call me or Jye."

I put a note I had written before this down on the counter with mine and Jye's numbers just in case he needed it. This was definitely not something I did for anyone but for Peter, I felt like I needed to.

Peter nodded and I turned to leave. My hand was on the doorknob as he cleared his throat.

"I don't know what is happening with my daughter and yourself," he said. "But please leave her alone. She means no harm, she's merely protecting me. She has the fire of her mother, I'm afraid."

It was an honest request, one I should have no issue delivering on but something about the way I hadn't been able to stop thinking about Teeghan today, proved to me that I probably wouldn't be able to stop.

"She leaves for London in a few weeks," he continued. "It surely would be better if she left without issue. I will have her apologize if she has slighted you in any way."

"It's fine, Peter," I said. "As you say, she'll be gone in a few weeks."

I left the shop as quickly as I could and got into my car. Shaking my head to clear it, I had no idea why the hell I felt so much anxiety about Teeghan leaving but I already knew I couldn't allow her to leave.

She was *mine*.

TEEGHAN

I FOLDED the letter again and stuffed it in my junk drawer. My divorce lawyer was relentless. I didn't get a fucking dime from my ex-husband, and I still didn't have a job in London to pay the fucker. My father wouldn't have any extra money to give me for doing the books, I was lucky enough to not have to pay for the apartment I was in due to it belonging to my aunt who was "discovering" herself in Africa. Looking back down at the laptop, and the spreadsheets I had open, trying to make my father's books digitized.

I wasn't even half done and I was leaving for London in ten days. I needed a stiff fucking drink.

Grabbing my coat, I headed out to get some fresh air. Divorcing the fuckwit was meant to make my life better, and yet I was further in debt than I was when I was with him. As I turned the corner, I headed toward the line of shops near the bay. That's when I saw the couple of men being intimidated with punches and uppercuts from men I recognized.

They were the men who had been with Conor at my father's shop when they shattered his door and now they were threatening some other poor guy.

Conor came out of the shop, putting his gun into his holster under his jacket. I spun around just as I saw Conor look up and over at me. Walking quickly back to my apartment, I prayed he didn't come after me.

But when I heard him running after me, I knew running would be useless. He knew where I lived, and he would probably have the strength to kick in my weak ass door.

I stopped walking and turned back around. He looked as intensely sexy as he did when he stood at my door after the shooting.

"Teeghan," he said. His voice was deep, menacing. "What did you see?"

"Nothing, really," I replied, my voice was relatively level. "I saw you talking to a few guys."

"Then why did you run away when you saw me?" he asked. "Is it because of this?"

He lifted his jacket to show me the gun in its holster.

"No, I've seen guns before," I told him, all the while trying to stop the throbbing from down below. Something about Conor and the danger that came associated with him had my pussy begging for another round with him.

"Then why did you run?"

"Oh, I don't know, maybe because you're an O'Farrell and everyone runs from you."

He smirked at me, and my pussy thrummed to life yet again. "You weren't scared the other night."

"Maybe I was," I replied, realizing he was flirting with me.

"You're too stubborn to admit that" he told me. That was true, usually I would never admit that but with Conor, I was different. What the hell was that?

"I thought you would be getting ready to go to London," he said.

"How did you know about that?"

"Your father told me," he said. "I went to visit him."

My heart began to race. "Why?"

"I can't tell you everything about me," he said with that devilish smirk yet again.

"So, it was illegal then," I said, feeling brave enough to joke.

"He told me to stay away from you," Conor said, the smirk dropping from his face. I could see he was battling some kind of inner demon.

"He did?"

"He would only do that if he thought you liked me."

Goddamn it, da.

"Well I did sleep with you, so that's a good guess."

Conor looked back at his men who were waiting for him in the car. He turned back to me.

"When do you leave?" he asked.

"Ten days."

"I gotta go," he said, before he turned and left me standing alone in the street. I must not have been breathing because I let out a deep breath that almost choked me once he drove off. Leaning against the brick wall, I tried to calm my breathing. Conor was looking at me like a treat, and damn it, I wanted him to eat me all night long.

Turning back around, I headed home to get stuck into the numbers, just a sad excuse to go home and take my mind off the way Conor was looking at me.

CONOR

Fuck.

Seeing Tee again was doing nothing for my throbbing cock. We'd fucked until we couldn't keep our eyes open the other night and I was looking for round two already. I never went back to the same woman, well not anymore anyway.

"She's trouble," Jakob said to me.

"Shut up, Jake," Jye shot at him as he sped toward the docks. The two guys were in the boot and were trying desperately to kick their way out. The sound was driving me nuts. I took my gun and shot through the back seat into the boot. A low grunt and scream erupted but then there was quiet.

Jakob and Jye both looked at me, waiting for me to crack but I simply shrugged.

"What? They were going to die anyway."

I didn't need Jakob talking down to me about a woman. He was my inferior, and he needed a damn reminder of that.

Teeghan was going to be a problem. Ten days and she would be gone. No one could fault me if I fucked that woman senseless, having those red curls bouncing atop her head as she mounted me and rode me for all she was worth until she left, right? Fuck it.

I already knew she wasn't going anywhere. I wouldn't let her.

She was fucking *mine* until I decided she wasn't anymore.

Jye pulled up at the docks and we got out. I waited for them to lug the idiots out of the trunk. The water had been still today, no waves to speak of, which wasn't uncommon but it made for an eerie night atmosphere.

Jye and Jakob pulled the men up and had them kneel in front of me. I pulled my gun free of its holster and held it loosely by my side. I saw who I'd shot in the car, his wound bleeding profusely, and he swayed as he tried to stay upright.

"How many are there?" I asked them. They hadn't answered me at the shop, but I was always one for second chances. Jakob kicked one of them in the back and he landed on his face on the hard ground. He grunted loudly as Jakob hauled him back up into a kneeling position. His mouth and nose were bleeding heavily.

"We don't know," the one who was shot said. "We're just pawns. You need to go after O'Brien."

"He's disappeared and I'm trying to track him down. Care to tell me where to find him?" I asked.

"Fuck you," said the nose bleeder.

I smirked at the fucker. "You're not my type. One more time, how many are involved?"

"We don't know," he spat. Blood splattering in front of him. "They'll overrun you and your brothers. The O'Farrell's are going down."

I held the gun up and shot the guy through the eyes. He fell back with the impact, blood spilling out of the wound and onto the ground.

The guy next to him shook with terror as I turned to him.

"If you don't know where he is, how about you tell me what they're planning?"

"They meet every fortnight. The next meeting is in two days. It's at the town hall."

I looked to Jye who nodded and ran inside to do his work.

"Was that so hard?" I asked him, as I raised my gun and shot him in the head. He went down quickly. Jakob moved over to cut the O with the roman numeral for three in the middle into his forehead. My calling card.

That would help spread fear when they washed up in a few days. And I would have a few days before the rebellion knew I was onto them.

"How goes the other two?" Jye asked me, joining us again just as the sound of the bodies hitting the water made a splash.

"Killian has them, so god only knows what they've had done to them."

Jye smirked, knowing just how crazy Killian could be. The

calm assassin as we called him. He was the calmest of all of us, and the most reckless, but he had a way of calming people into a false sense of hope and then blasting their entire life wide open.

"Speaking of," I said. "I need to meet up with him."

Jye nodded as I headed toward the car and took off for the town center again. Getting out, I ran up the stairs of the church and walked down the aisle to where Killian stood with Father Murphy. I joined them and noticed Father Murphy's weary expression. He hated the crime in this town, but he also loved us. He and my father had been best friends in school, so he'd kept us clean and protected most of our lives.

I was still religious.

Lorcan wasn't. He'd never step foot in here again, not after losing his girlfriend years ago.

"Father."

"Conor, I heard rumors of two of our former usher boys being kidnapped in broad daylight earlier," he said. "You wouldn't know anything about that, would you?"

"I recall you telling me never to tell you the dealings I have in my everyday life," I said. "Unless we were in a confessional."

He rolled his eyes which made Killian and I both laugh just as we heard the doors open. A familiar woman walked in and stopped when she saw us. She obviously didn't want to see us and so she backed away and left in a hurry. I turned back to Father Murphy who was looking at Killian.

That's when I saw it.

Killian looked gutted, like he'd been sucker punched.

"Who the hell was that?" I asked. "And why does she look so familiar?"

"Her name is Sloane," Father Murphy said.

I turned back to Killian. "*The* Sloane?"

"Is that all you needed from me, Father?" Killian stood and walked away without so much as a goodbye.

"Damn that woman did a number on him," I said.

"That is what love does," Father Murphy said. "Now, I want to know how you are going with the containers coming in from Italy."

"They're on track to arrive in a few days," I said. "What's in there, Father? You've never used my services before."

"It's private," he said. "The Lord and I have an agreement and that's all you need to know."

"Keep your secrets, Father," I said. "I'll have Jye call you when it comes in."

I turned on my heel and left.

I had nothing else on my plate for the day and there was only one thing I wanted to do since I saw her earlier.

I drove to Teeghan's apartment and parked around the corner before heading up the stairs and knocking on her door.

No answer.

I grabbed my lock pick from my wallet and broke into the apartment, closing the door behind me quickly. The apartment was clear, boxes lining the floor in the study. I looked around to see what was lying around. I had no idea why I cared so much but for some reason, I couldn't kick Teeghan out of my mind, and it was driving me crazy.

Opening her cupboards in the kitchen, I saw hardly anything in there. She really was leaving. I pulled open her drawers and found a stack of letters in there.

I fought back the smile. My mother had done that, hid the letters in a drawer so she didn't have to deal with it. Pulling out the one on top, I unfolded it and read the letter of demand from a lawyer. She needed to pay her divorce lawyer and judging by the tone of the letter it was overdue. I took a photo of the lawyer's name with my phone and put the letter back. I picked up a lined piece of paper which was folded in two and opened it.

It was a note from a guy, presumably her ex-husband. Everything in me told me not to read it but I couldn't help myself.

Teeghan,

Never did I think you would be such a selfish whore. You know I just want to move on and be happy, and yeah I probably shouldn't have done it the way I did but I just want you to move on and leave me and Emma alone. We deserve to be happy. You never even liked being here, you were always thinking about Ireland. Just fucking sign the paperwork and let me marry the woman I love.

Fuck - I just want to be done with you and your bullshit.

Sign it before I have to come to Ireland and force you to sign it.

I never thought I would hate someone I'd never met. No matter what she had done to him, speaking to her like this was cowardly. He obviously left her to be with another woman which made him the scum of the universe.

I opened the letter from her lawyer again and scanned

for his name so I could find this motherfucker but he wasn't listed. Instead, I looked at the letter he had sent her and there in the corner, I saw the watermark on the stationery. He'd sent the letter from his office stationery.

What a dumbass.

Shoving both the letters away, I took a seat on her sofa and waited for her to come home, my cock at the ready.

TEEGHAN

THE RAIN HAD BEEN both cold and hard as I ran through the streets toward my apartment. Since when had it been forecast for rain? It was such a lovely day today.

God.

The one time I had wanted to enjoy the day without driving around and it does this to me. I ran up the steps of my apartment building and up the stairs. A nice, warm shower was going to do wonders for me after that bout and then I'd down half a bottle of whiskey before settling in to watch whatever movie was on the TV. I opened my door but felt a strange sensation I wasn't used to. It felt like someone was watching me. I closed the door and grabbed the knife I kept on the top of my kitchen bench.

That's when I saw him.

Standing by my sliding doors that led out onto my balcony.

"What the fuck are you doing in here?" I rounded on him.

That devilish smirk appeared on his face again, and my knees wobbled a little. What the actual fuck? That was a thing and not some cliched action a woman did in romance novels? Knees could wobble at a smirk?

"Are you going to stab me?" he asked, his voice deep and sexy as all get out.

"I'm contemplating it."

"What happened to the fun, flirty Teeghan from before?"

"She hadn't just been rained on and had a shitty day."

"Rain can make you this unhappy?" he asked.

"Rain is not the problem. The problem is you being in my apartment when it was locked."

He made his way over to me, and I felt my hand shake around the knife hilt. I could smell his masculine cologne, and my head felt like it was spinning. His hands made their way to my face, cupping it before he pressed his lips to mine. The kiss was slow, sensual, and had all my anger seeping away. The knife fell from my grip, clattering on the tiles, as I wound my arm around his neck. He pulled me closer to him, pressing my body up against his rock hard abs and causing me to moan into his mouth.

He pushed me up against the kitchen counter but it was too high for him to put me up there. Instead, he pulled back and started to pull the wet clothes from my body. My skin felt clammy and gross. Conor took my hand, and led me to my bathroom, where he continued to undress me. His eyes were on mine the entire time, their intensity never wavering. I could feel my body shaking and not because I was cold. He turned on the taps and tested the water before he put me under the warm spray. The instant the water hit my cold and clammy body, I instantly felt relief. The warm water was heating me up, my pussy thrumming to life at being so close to Conor.

He stripped down and stepped into the shower stall with me. His lips claimed mine again, as his arms wrapped around my waist. The water made it easy for his hands to slip down over my ass and cup it. He slapped my cheek and I made a yelping sound against his lips. I could feel his smirk appear against my lips. Conor pushed me up against the tiled wall, the hard coolness against my back was a direct opposite to the warm water cascading over my body and the heat generating from being in such close proximity to Conor. The way he looked me up and down had my pussy clenching. He looked like he wanted to eat me.

And I would not be opposed to that in the least. His hand roamed down between us and a solitary finger slid down to my pussy, pushing in to prod at my clit, I wanted to scream as he ran his calloused fingertip over the tight little button of nerves. He moved his finger down further until I could feel him inside of me, playing with the sides of my pussy walls with that cheeky finger. His mouth was on my neck, playing with that little spot right under the ear. The spot that made my knees go literally weak. I struggled to keep standing as the pleasure lapped over me with ferocity. He held me up, somehow, and I let my head rest against the cool tiles behind me. The bathroom was steaming up but we were barely under the water. His hair was wet, but he'd swept it backward, beads of water clung to his face and neck, enticing me to suck them off him. Conor began to move into me with a faster pace, pushing another finger inside to widen me.

All thoughts of the bad day had been lifted and my sole focus was on Conor right now. I wrapped my arms around his neck as he hammered his fingers into me. I needed to hold on for dear life or I'd slip in the water pooling around my feet. His fingers created a whirlpool of sensation down below as the water beat down on Conor's back and over my arms. I was in heaven.

My breathing became shallow and I struggled to keep

my feet on the ground as his fingers took me over the edge. I screamed out his name, right in his ear as he pounded his fingers into me, pushing my orgasm out. My hips gyrating over his fingers as I rode the waves of pleasure.

Once they subsided, I felt my body go almost limp in the warm water. Conor turned the taps off, keeping me draped over him as he pulled a towel from the rack and wrapped it around me.

It was so soft, his actions not at all what I would expect. It felt like he was taking care of me. Not even my ex had been like this for me, not even when I had pneumonia and had almost died. Conor claimed my mouth again and all of a sudden, I was reinvigorated. My strength returned and I kissed him back just as hard. Conor pushed me out the door and toward the bedroom. The animal was back after the momentary thoughtfulness and I could see him coming to take his prey. I was both excited and determined to make him mine in the next bout. As I dropped the towel and stepped back so he could take a good look at what I had on offer, I watched as his eyes raked up and down my body. I was a little self-conscious but hell, he'd seen it all before, and he was back for more, so I knew there was nothing to worry about.

He closed the distance between us quickly, taking me by the neck with one hand and squeezing. I could feel the intensity in his eyes shoot all the way down my back and toward my pussy.

God, how could he make me feel this way every single damn time?

He pushed me down on the bed and kicked my knees apart so I was spread eagled on the edge of the bed. He knelt down and grabbed my thighs, pulling them up over his shoulders. I had no time to react before his mouth was on my pussy, his tongue slipping in between my lips and teasing my clit. I grabbed onto the edge of the bed and dropped my shoulders back so I could drive my head into the mattress. He hit the spot every damn time.

My hips were moving frantically but he put his arm down over them, giving him more room to wiggle his tongue around my clit and cause vibrations up and down my pussy that had me clutching at the sheets, and gasping for air. He slid two fingers into me at the same time as his tongue prodded and tickled my clit and I felt my pussy clamp down around his fingers as my orgasm hit me suddenly. I screamed his name which only made him grunt as I bucked my hips with every spasm. Once the waves ebbed, I laid back on the bed, my legs still on his shoulders as he placed kisses on the sides of my legs.

It didn't last long.

He flipped me so I was laying on top of him, straddling him. I could feel his hard cock against my ass cheeks as I looked down at him, realizing I was in complete control now.

"Quit smiling and fuck me," he growled. I took my time, moving my hand underneath me and grabbing hold of his thick pole, sliding my hand up and down it. He hissed out a deep breath as he watched me. His mouth set in two thin white lines as he tried everything in his power not to take over. I could see his restraint was straining against his desire to have me do what I want to him.

It was huge that he was giving me control.

Massive.

I doubted a guy like Conor would ever give that up for any woman. The thought of him with other women, even though I knew it would be the case, had my stomach burning. Conor was the hottest guy in town. Of course, he had his pick of women. Why then did it feel like I was sucker punched when I thought of him with another woman?

I positioned his cock and slid the tip inside of me. Conor moved his head back as he took deep breaths at how achingly slow I was going.

If I wanted to keep this up, I needed to show him I was the only woman who could make him feel this way. I needed to show up these other whores he'd been with and be the only one he ever wanted to be with from now on.

I moved my ass up again until he was almost all the way out of me and then I slammed myself back down quickly.

He jolted his head up, his eyes wide and his mouth in an O. His eyes looked so dark in this moment, that I thought I may just cum right here and now. I loved the way he looked like a beast in the throes of passion.

I pushed him back down, my hands splayed over his pecs to keep him there as I moved my hips up and down, my pussy polishing that cock of his three ways to Sunday. His hands flew to my hips, to try and control me but I swatted them away. He threw his hands back on the bed, under a pillow to stop the temptation. I missed his fingertips digging into the flesh over my hips though. I loved the pain that ratchet up my spine when he did it. It just showed how much he loved having me ride him.

I watched as his face contorted into pleasure and surprise as I moved my hips around at different angles. I could feel his cock getting harder inside of me. That was something I'd never felt before with any man. Conor pushed up, grabbing my neck and pulling me down for a soul stealing kiss.

A kiss that promised more. A kiss that told me he wanted me.

I pushed him back down and rode him harder and

faster. Bouncing on top of him as he watched my breasts bounce with me. His eyes on mine as I saw him tense up. He was close.

I bore down on him like an avalanche as he tensed again, his hands flying to my hips and digging in hard. My own pussy was clenching around him from just the pain from his fingertips in my skin. I screamed out just as he called out my name and I felt him cum into me.

Once our breathing returned to normal, I collapsed against him. His sweaty chest didn't bother me as I laid my head down on him and closed my eyes, relishing the feel of what we'd just done. I rolled off him and onto my side, my eyes were closing as I felt him pull me against him.

CHAPTER SEVEN

TEEGHAN

I heard my phone ringing from the living room, and I instantly looked to the other side of the bed to see if Conor was still there but the side he'd fallen asleep on was empty. I moved out to the living room and looked at my phone which had three missed calls from Sloane and several texts. I called her back.

"Hey," she said, almost exasperated. "Where have you been?"

"Sorry, I must have slept in."

"How did the job interview go?" she asked me. It had been the reason I'd had such a monumental bad day. I'd even gone to the park to take the phone interview because I felt better in the open air when I was nervous. By the end of the call I knew I didn't get the job. I had eight days to get my shit into gear before I left for London and I still had no place to stay or even a job to go to.

Time was running out.

"No go," I said. "I'm starting to believe I'll never get out of here."

"It will happen," she said. "There's no use in sleeping in until noon."

I checked the clock on my microwave and saw that it was in fact just past noon. How the hell had that happened?

"You're right," I said to her, not wanting to let on that I'd been with Conor again. "I might go to the gym and work off some of this anger."

"You do that, love."

She hung up and I went into the bathroom to have a shower before I left. Memories flooded back of what we did in here the night before and immediately I felt a little hot. I turned on the taps and got under the spray, washing off quickly before I jumped out and got dressed in my workout gear. A large crop top and lycra three quarter length pants. I grabbed my keys and my workout bag and headed down the stairs. I decided to forgo the car and walked down to the gym on the corner. The walk would do me good. Thoughts of Conor, memories of the night before and the anxiety of not having anywhere to go next was causing me to panic.

The only way to get this crushing anxiety out of me was to work it off. I'd had similar attacks when I was in London, and my ex had put it down to me being too emotional. One of the reasons he claimed he had fucked off with my best friend Emma. She had her hormones in control, or so he said. I knew better but I would rather he find out the hard way himself.

As I turned the corner, I saw Conor's men standing out the front of a bar talking to a man. It seemed friendly enough, there were no weapons drawn and no one was being threatened.

One of them who I saw with Conor all the time noticed

me. I couldn't see Conor with them so I wondered if he was inside. He jogged over to me, crossing the street. I didn't know whether to run or to stay put. My heart was hammering in my chest until he got to me.

"Teeghan, right?"

I nodded.

"I'm Jye," he said with a smile. "Conor had to go out of town for a few days."

"Oh," I replied, wondering why he was telling me unless Conor wanted me to know. Why didn't he just tell me? "Ok sure."

"Did you want his number?" he asked me, pulling his phone out. That was the question, wasn't it? Could I be trusted with his digits? What if I got drunk one night and decided to use it?

"No, it's okay. You can just tell him to come and see me when he gets back."

Jye nodded. "Sure."

I was about to walk up the stairs to the gym when I turned back before I knew what I was doing.

"Actually, yeah, give it to me."

Jye smirked at me, just like Conor did. Only, I wasn't attracted to Jye, so it only irritated me. I quickly copied the digits of Conor's number into my phone and thanked Jye.

"Hey," he called out to me before I could run back up the stairs. "Take my number too. In case you need it when he's not around. If you're ever in trouble, just call me and I'll come and help you."

"Why would I be in trouble?" I asked.

"Look, people have noticed Conor's attraction to you. He has enemies. I'm not one to scare people but if you felt you needed assistance, call me."

I realized he was offering it because Conor's obsession

with me hadn't gone unnoticed by people in town. It wouldn't be such a bad idea to have back up especially since I didn't know anyone else other than Sloane to call in town.

"Okay."

He showed me the number and I entered it into my phone. He headed across the street and I took the steps up to the gym, feeling heavy about the situation.

Would I be in trouble here now? Would my dad?

I put my gym bag in the locker and headed out to the treadmill. Putting my earphones in, I started to walk. I tried to clear my mind of what the fuck just happened and the fact that Conor was out of town just hours after he left my bed without a word.

What the fuck was happening?

What was I involved in?

As I continued to walk, I watched as a group of skinny minnie girls walked past me in their crop tops that looked like bras and their mini shorts where you could totally see ass cheeks out the bottom and whispered to themselves. I could see their little bitchy glares as they walked past, talking about me. As I turned around, I could see everyone was looking at me.

Everyone.

Even the men were looking at me, but not in a good way.

"What?!" I exploded.

Everyone turned back to what they were doing and ignored me. I had one of the personal trainers come over to me, the stern looks on his face told me this wasn't going to be a good conversation.

"I think it's best if you leave, miss."

"Why?"

"We don't want your kind in here, it's causing our clients to become agitated."

"I didn't do anything to your *clients*," I said with air quotes at the end, just to be a bitch.

"Look, I don't want to call the police, just go."

I pulled my earphones out, even though I hadn't had a chance to blast my music yet and stepped off the treadmill. This was to do with Conor.

I knew it.

That only made me angrier.

"You're going to regret this."

He stiffened a little, the snarkiness gone from his expression as he realized I could really fuck his shit up if I wanted to.

I doubted Conor would raze a gym for mistreating me. Fuck, I doubted he would even care. I was a sometime fuck buddy and that was it.

My heart hammered in my chest as I pushed past him and went to retrieve my bag. As I was heading for the door, I saw the skinny minnie cross her arms and huff.

"Watch out, guys, give her a wide berth," she said. "This one's got some weight on her."

Her friends laughed as I passed, and I stopped in my tracks and dropped my bag. I knew I wasn't fat, if anything I had a little bit of chub and that was it. I was still fit as a horse. But that was neither here nor there, she was the reason people who needed to come to the gym didn't. They were judged.

Fuck her.

Even if I were fat, you didn't fucking say shit about it.

Without missing a beat, I marched over to her and clocked her across the face. She screamed as she stumbled back, clutching her nose.

"Bitch," I said as I grabbed my bag and left the gym. I was out the door so fast, tears threatening as I took a deep breath of fresh air. Jye was crossing the street again, a look of concern on his face.

"You okay?" he asked me. "You weren't there for long."

"I got kicked out."

"Why?"

"I guess because they don't want to be associated with Conor."

"I'll talk to them."

"It doesn't matter," I told him. "I don't care. It was only to take my mind off shit anyway. I'll go for a run around the park."

Just as I was about to walk off, skinny minnie came out, clutching her bleeding nose, her bottle blonde hair slightly pink at the ends from the blood. She was screeching, being held up by the personal trainer and her friends. She saw me standing there, fighting to keep the smile off my face as they tried to lead her away. She pushed them off her and she came over to me. Her nose looked a little wonky which made me smile.

"You bitch."

"Careful, wouldn't want me to attack something else cosmetically enhanced of yours," I said, looking down at her enormous breasts. Her friends gasped as she looked at me in horror.

"I think it's best if you shoved off, Makenna."

She shot Jye a warning look before she flipped her hair over her shoulder and marched back off to join her friends. They headed for the carpark.

"Watch yourself, Brian," I heard Jye say to the personal trainer as he moved back inside. He did look as if he'd shit himself as he did it though.

"Nice," Jye said to me with a chuckle. "I don't think anyone's ever given Makenna any lip back in her entire life. You just made my day."

"Who is she?" I asked.

Jye hesitated for a moment, but I already knew before she said it. "She's Conor's ex."

Great.

Just fucking perfect. I was up against Barbie over there. If he didn't want to be with her, what the hell chance did I have?

CONOR

I WAITED outside the law office of Teeghan's lawyer. He had a small practice, and it appeared only he and his assistant were working today. That was good for me. After flying to London after my hunt for Paul turned up nothing, I didn't really know why I'd come here until I found myself standing here, waiting for the perfect time to bust in on this asshole.

After half an hour of standing here, looking sus as fuck, his assistant left the office. I ran across the street and entered the office. I moved through the reception area and into the office with the fat fucker.

He pushed back on his chair and made a move to grab a weapon from under his desk. I pulled my gun free quickly. He held both his hands up, the panic trickling in.

"Who are you?" he asked me.

"I've come to discuss a client with you."

"I can't discuss my clients."

"I think you'll make an exception here," I said to him, sitting down, while keeping the gun trained on him.

"My assistant will return shortly and she'll call the police."

"Good point," I said. I got up and closed the door to his office and sat back down, retraining the gun on him. "Thanks for that."

"Based on your accent I can already tell who you've come for," he said, his tone telling me I wasn't going to like what he was about to say about Teeghan. "And all I can say is she needs to pay."

"I don't think she does."

"Look, it's sad what happened to her but that's divorce. It's a nasty business-"

"Sure does make you a lot of coin, though, doesn't it?"

He sat back in his chair, and tried to contain whatever he wanted to tell me. I wish he would. I wish he'd give me all the reason in the world to put a bullet between his eyes but that wouldn't help anyone right now.

"Why'd she lose everything in the divorce?" I asked him.

"Her ex is a goddamn lawyer. He knew exactly what he'd need before she even bothered to divorce the lout. I'm sorry for her, I am, but I still did her a service. I need to be paid and I've given her enough extensions."

This guy wasn't going to relent, and truthfully, he was right. He did do her a service but I knew she wasn't going to be able to pay. There was no way her father was paying for her looking after his books so I had to do something to help her.

I pulled an envelope from my back pocket and tossed it over to him. "This should cover it."

He opened it and looked at the bills inside. "This definitely covers it."

"Good, one more thing," I said, putting my gun away. "I need the ex's home address."

"I can't do that."

"I'm sure you can," I said. He hesitated for a moment before he finally relented and pulled open his drawer. He flipped through some paperwork and finally found the page he was looking for. He wrote down the address and handed it to me.

"You didn't get this from me."

I smiled as I walked to the door.

"Whatever you think you've just done for her, be careful. She's a wreck and she may just pull you down with her."

The anger that had subsided was back again as I turned back around. "That's a little hasty to say, isn't it?"

"She's been a mess for a long time, she just hides it well."

"Maybe you just don't know her well enough," I bit back, angrier than ever. I moved out of the office before I did something I would regret. I stopped as I was at the door and turned around and headed back inside. He was looking down at his paperwork, his hand over his phone as he frantically typed away. I grabbed the closest thing I could see. A letter opener.

I slammed the pointy end down into his hand on the desk, causing a scream to emit from his nasty mouth.

"Who are you texting?"

I looked down and saw the name above the number. It was Andrew Potter. The name I recognized from the ex's letterhead.

He was going to warn him.

I smashed the phone onto the ground and slammed my foot down on it. I let go of the letter opener and took a step back.

He was still groaning, his other hand holding the wound around the letter opener as he looked up at me in horror.

"You shouldn't have done that."

"What are you going to do now?" he asked in rasps.

"Unless you get medical help soon, you'll bleed out and honestly, I've never thought of anything more enjoyable than to watch that but since I'm on borrowed time in London, I'll speed the process up."

"What?"

"You dissed my woman," I said to him, liking how it felt to call Teeghan my woman. "All you had to do was keep your filthy trap shut."

He tried to pull the letter opener off his hand, but it was hurting him too much. I grabbed him by the neck as I walked behind him, and I held his head up so he was looking at me as I pulled my gun free and held the barrel next to his head. He was sobbing and pleading with me as I let go of his neck and took the shot. His body jerked for a moment before he slumped in his chair.

Grabbing the envelope of cash, I pocketed it again and closed the office door. I was just leaving through the front door when the assistant came up.

"Have a nice day."

I walked off as she smiled at me and headed inside. I took off, hailing a cab before she found her boss in his office and headed to the apartment of Andrew Potter.

My phone dinged and I looked down at Jye's message. Father Murphy's container had finally arrived.

A man like the priest knew everyone's bad secrets, he

knew everything that went on in the community whether he wanted to or not.

He had to know more about the O'Brien's.

I texted back to tell him to hold off on telling Murphy until I was back.

I had just figured out a way to end this rebellion right from the core, and I had the perfect tactic to get Murphy to give me exactly what we needed to get this goddamn rebellion ended once and for all.

THE APARTMENT WAS nice and clean. Cleaner than I thought possible for a man but then I knew he had a woman who was probably nothing like Teeghan. Her apartment had been anything but clean, but it hadn't been too messy. Just enough to make it look like she actually lived in it. This apartment though, this could be a display apartment. I looked around for anything personal, or something I could use to beat the ever living crap out of the asshole who broke Teeghan's heart with.

I stood by the window, against the backdrop of expensive curtains that looked heavy enough they could kill me if they fell on me and waited.

I didn't have to wait long. A waft of expensive and entirely too fruity perfume came my way. I did everything to stave off the gagging. Why did women think having expensive perfume meant you had to spray it fucking everywhere?

She moved past me without noticing me standing there and into the kitchen. It was a small kitchen, one that wasn't used for the normal dinners but rather to serve canapes for their fancy friends. She was grabbing a wine glass and pulled up a bottle from a bottom cabinet. As she poured, I could see she was uncomfortable. She could sense I was here but she hadn't bothered to look my way. I was a master at hiding until I wanted to be seen. Even as a kid, I used to listen in on conversations my parents really didn't want me to know. To this day, I knew things about my family that my own brothers didn't. She moved over to the bench and eyed the super sharp knives in the holder but she didn't grab one.

Dumb decision, lady.

As she made her way out of the kitchen, she shook her head as if she was shaking away the stupid fears she'd been having and headed toward me. She hadn't seen me yet which was great, the element of surprise was always my favorite. As she moved past me, I grabbed her by the neck and launched her back against the floor to ceiling window. Her red wine spilled out over her fancy white carpet and the glass fell to the ground as she gasped, looking up at me wide eyed and fearful. I walked her over to the chair I had moved to the side of the room which she hadn't noticed and tied her hands behind her back with the rope I'd brought with me.

"Who are you?" she asked, sobbing. "Take whatever you want and leave."

"This isn't about money, love," I told her. "You're not who I'm here for."

"Drew? What's he done? Did he represent you?" she asked, trying to come to terms with what was happening to her. I'd seen it before. She was going to turn hysterical in about five minutes if I didn't do something.

"Just shut up and wait," I told her. I pulled the scarf I'd taken from their bedroom earlier and pulled it through her lips and tied it at the back. She tried to scream but it was muted enough that she couldn't get any sound out. Tears rolled down her cheeks, marking her face with the piles of makeup she had on. I could see the black lined tears on her cheeks already.

I sat down at the table and waited for Andrew to show his face. I told her to keep quiet or I'd start shooting her feet. It had kept her relatively quiet while I waited. The phone rang and the answering machine picked it up.

"Thanks for calling Andrew and Em. We can't come to the phone right now so leave us a message."

I rolled my eyes at the boring message and waited for the person to speak.

"Em, it's me. Why aren't you home yet? You know I like it when you're home before me. I'm running late so hopefully you will be home by then. Can you order me food?"

He hung up. What a fucking jerk.

"Well, I guess we've got more time to ourselves, *Em*."

She started to sob again and pull against her ties.

"I wouldn't," I told her. "My dad taught me if you're going to tie someone up, you need to do it so they never escape. I was always an attentive son."

She stopped trying to move her arms, probably because the ropes would be causing friction burns on her wrists by now and they fucking hurt.

I got up and looked around the apartment for something to do while we waited. As much as I could sit and be unnoticed for hours if needed, I wanted to do something, get to know the man who broke Teeghan's heart. I pulled open a drawer under the bureau near the living room and rifled through the contents.

Bills, boring letters and documents. Moving through the living room, I found a bunch of stuff hidden under the coffee table but nothing proved to be exciting there either. Next, I moved on to the other side, where a makeshift desk stood against the wall. I looked through the papers, finding a cache of stuff I probably shouldn't see. He was obviously a criminal lawyer, and I could see prisoner files and police records meaning he was a defense lawyer.

Interesting.

As I pulled open the filing cabinet, I saw a small wooden box at the bottom of the cabinet. The files probably hid it most of the time, but they'd all been pushed back at some point and I could clearly see it. I pulled it out and looked over at Emma. Her eyebrows knit together in confusion as I opened the latch.

She'd obviously not seen it before which meant this was going to be fun. I opened the latch and looked down at the contents. A photo sat on the top of a younger Teeghan. Immediately my jealousy sprung up. I felt it burning a hole in my chest. She looked happy in the photo and so did he. I couldn't tell how long ago it was but there was definite love there.

I held the photo up so she could see it. Her eyes widened but she sat back in the chair and looked elsewhere.

"I guess he's not over his ex, huh?"

She refused to look back over at me. Hmm, I should leave Andrew to his precious new fiancée. She'd probably do a better job than I ever could.

I didn't think I came here to kill him but I didn't want him thinking he could ever have Teeghan back and judging from this photo that he kept hidden away, that's precisely what he had on his mind.

I flicked through the rest of the box and saw trinkets and wedding rings, and a photo of Teeghan alone. She was standing in the middle of a field of lilies and on the back of the photo was the date and the words "Day of Sean's funeral". These were the lilies that she had tattooed on her ankle.

She hadn't come back to Ireland for his funeral. I wondered why. I put the box back in the cabinet and ripped up the photo and threw the pieces over the floor.

I pulled down the gag she had on. "Did you know her?"

"This is about Teeghan?"

"Answer my question."

"Yes, I knew her. She was–"

She stopped speaking and looked into my eyes, fearful of what I may say. I knew I wasn't going to like what she said.

"Yes?"

"She was my best friend."

"And you stole her husband?"

"She wasn't giving him the attention he needed. She wasn't a good wife to him, she was always crying, always sad."

"And the thing to do in that case is sleep with her husband? Did you ever think she needed her friend to help her?"

Emma looked away from me, obviously realizing how bad a person she was.

"Once a cheater, always a cheater," I said. "You know that right?"

"You telling me you haven't ever cheated on a woman?" she asked me.

"I've never dated a woman to cheat on," I told her, kneeling so I could get close to her. I could feel the tension on her, feel the stiffness in her body as she tried to look anywhere but at me.

"Why are you here then? Did she send you?"

"Actually, no," I said, realizing Teeghan would be pretty

mad if I told her I had come here. She seemed like a pretty private person who wanted to handle her own shit. "She'll probably rake my ass over the coals if she found out."

The fear on Emma's face told me it all. "You're going to kill us, aren't you?"

"The thought had crossed my mind."

I pushed the scarf back into her mouth and tied it tighter. She started to sob again, as the realization this may be her last few moments alive hit her. I made my way over to the table where I had been sitting before, stewing over the fact that this fucker had designs on my woman.

He wanted her back because he realized the woman he was with was lacking.

Well, fuck him.

He couldn't have her.

She was mine.

The keys jangled outside the door. I looked at Emma who looked at the door, full of hope. I got off the chair and moved into the darkness. The one area that wasn't lit up by the dimmed lights.

"Em, you home?" he called out as he closed the door. He looked down at the side table and put his keys down before he walked in, shucking off his shoes before he looked up and saw Emma desperate to get his attention.

"What the fuck?" he said as he looked around. Instead of going to her immediately like I thought he would, he was searching for a weapon. He must keep a gun somewhere close because he was edging around, looking for me. I fired off a shot, luckily the silencer would keep the noise to a minimum. He ducked and fell to the ground, but I knew I hadn't hit him. I was a skilled marksman, I didn't need blood to tell me if I had hit a target or not.

"Get up," I called out to him. "I would have assumed you'd go to untie your lover over there first."

He stood up, looking over at me for the first time, with defiance.

"If you were going to hurt her, you would have done it already."

"Not necessarily. It really does depend on how annoying you're going to be and right now, as I look at you, I can see you're going to be superbly annoying."

"Who are you and why the fuck are you in my home?" he asked me.

"Who I am doesn't matter, and I came here because I was curious."

"About what?"

"About a man who could give up someone as fine as Teeghan and think this piece of trash on the chair would ever be good enough."

His face changed instantly. He looked briefly at Emma before he straightened himself and looked back at me. "This is about Teeghan?"

"Obviously."

"You're with her now? She sent you here?"

"No, she didn't. I was curious and happened to be in the area."

"Well, you've found out now. You can fuck off back to Ireland."

"Before I go," I said. "Just a question, why the fuck would you leave her penniless?"

He looked over at Emma who had her eyebrows pushed down as if she were confused. I moved over to her, keeping my gun trained on him, and lifted the scarf off her mouth.

"You told me you paid her that money," she shot at him. "You left her penniless after everything you did to her?"

"Shut up, Em."

"No, Emma, don't shut up, do go on."

"He was supposed to pay her like ten grand. He told me he would. It was to say sorry for how it all shaped up."

"Because of your friendship."

Emma nodded, fresh tears making their way down her face.

"Well, doesn't that make you a fresh dick," I turned to him.

"Get out of my apartment," he said, gathering some fresh courage. "I'll have security here in two minutes."

"Hardly," I told him. "I got past your so-called security quite easily. I hardly doubt they'll leave their football match to come up here."

"What do you want?" he asked me.

"I don't really know, now that I've seen you, I'm completely underwhelmed and that doesn't happen often."

Andrew started to laugh. "Oh, I see. She's trapped you into wanting her, right? She's not someone you want to get messed up with, trust me."

I felt my heart rate plummet yet again. "For someone who wants her back, you certainly do have an odd way of showing it."

"I never said that."

"Exes don't keep memories like in that little box for nothing," I said. Raising my gun, I shot into his shoulder. He screamed out and fell to the ground, clutching his wound. He looked up at me in shock. He obviously didn't think I was going to shoot him but now he was crawling up against the back wall, bleeding.

"Fine," he called out. "I wanted her back. She was... different but she's just wild. She won't conform to being a lawyer's wife, so I thought I'd do better with someone conservative but to be honest...Em is just boring."

Emma gasped in shock and then I saw the anger appear. That had to hurt. Andrew was a real piece of shit. I walked over to him, keeping my gun trained on him until I got to where he was sitting. He was visibly shaking as he looked up at me.

He knew what I was going to do.

I wanted him to live in that fear for a few moments.

I wanted him to suffer.

A stream of pee started to mark the floorboards he was sitting on which made me chuckle. They all peed or shit themselves this close to death.

When he looked up at me, to see if I was only kidding, I took the shoot. The hole between his eyes wasn't huge but it was obviously a bullet hole. He had fallen back against the wall, his eyes wide open.

I turned back to Emma who was now sobbing but she didn't call out, she didn't scream to her credit. She had had more balls than Andrew ever did.

I aimed the gun at her head but I didn't pull the trigger. It wasn't like me to hesitate but for some reason, I knew she was just as much a victim of Andrew than Teeghan was. I lowered the gun and she looked up at me, with horror in her eyes.

"Why?"

"You're coming with me to Ireland."

"I don't–"

"Believe me, lady, you don't want to know what goes on in my mind. If you stay here, you'll be blamed for this."

She looked over at Andrew's body and slowly she shook her head. "Okay."

"Get cleaned up and grab a bag of clothes."

I untied her hands and watched her as she gathered her things. She didn't once try to sneak her phone into the bag. She had washed the tears off her face and now looked fresh and makeup free. She'd changed her clothes and now wore sweats and a band tee. She'd swapped her heels for a pair of sneakers. Her phone lay on the bed with the rest of the contents of her bag. She'd picked a few things from the bag but I knew it was more of an effort to show me she didn't want to try and deceive me.

"You're not taking the phone?"

"No need," she said. "For one thing, you wouldn't let me take it, but mostly, I don't have anyone else to call or text on it. No one talks to me anymore since I took up with Andrew."

She walked past me and into the living room. As we headed for the door, she looked down at Andrew's body and with a swift kick to the ribs, she walked out of the apartment. It had been surprising but I would have done worse to him if I were her. I led her down to the elevator bay. We rode down in silence. When I cast an eye over to her, I could see she was shaking slightly.

She was in shock.

The doors opened and we walked right past the security without so much as a word. I hailed a cab and we both got in. Still silent, I wondered what the hell I was going to do with her in Ireland.

I had always been impulsive and it had been bad for everyone around me but now I had a person, one who hurt my woman no less, and no idea what to do about it. I pulled my phone out and texted Jye.

CONOR

I'm bringing extra luggage home. Need a place for her to stay.

JYE

On it.

Jye never questioned my motives. Never. He was loyal as fuck, and I trusted him more than I did my own brothers. I wouldn't have a business if it weren't for that fucker.

As the cab pulled up at the private airfield, I saw her frown in confusion possibly before she looked at me.

"I don't fly commercial."

She nodded and got out with me. As we headed to the building where I knew our associate was, I looked over at the private plane waiting for us. It looked ready.

In just under two hours, I'd be home and I could get back to trying to convince Teeghan to stay in Ireland.

※

Jye was waiting for us when we arrived at the airport. The flight had been a rocky one. Although we were in luxury, it still didn't help the fact I hated flying. Emma was walking behind me, nervously. She'd been quiet the entire flight.

"Jye," I said. "This is Emma."

He held his hand out for Emma's bag and hefted it over his shoulder.

"Your brothers want you to see them at the estate as soon as you can make it," he told me. "It sounds urgent."

"Perfect."

He handed me the keys to the car and took Emma. He'd

probably already had a place set up to keep her while I figured out what to do about her. I got in behind the wheel and took off toward the estate.

I knew this was going to have to be about Teeghan. I could feel it already and after the day I've had, I didn't want to have to go through this but ignoring a request at the table wasn't exactly something we did.

"Nice of you to join us."

I pushed down the anger at Lorcan, so I didn't reach across and fuck him up.

"Just got back half an hour ago."

"Ah yes," Lorcan said, leaning back in the highchair dad always sat at. "The last-minute trip to London. What business did you have there?"

"You don't need to know that," I said. "It was personal."

"Since when do you have personal business in London?" Killian asked.

"What do you want?" I asked them both, already bored with the conversation. I had things to do.

"We need to know what Teeghan Kennedy knows about the family business."

I looked at Killian, wondering what the hell he was asking. He was dead serious, and when he was serious, it was never good.

"She doesn't know anything. Why are you asking me about her?"

My anger was mounting inside. I didn't like where he was going with this. I didn't like her name on his lips.

"Look, I know when a woman is making someone do stupid things. I know you went to London for her, so obviously things are a little more serious than just a fling."

"Get bent," I said, standing up.

"Sit down, Conor," Lorcan said. "We need to talk about this."

"Are you two jealous? You're both without women, you can't stand that I'm getting a little piece of ass?"

"A little piece of ass?" Lorcan repeated. "Is that all she is? You wouldn't mind her leaving to go and live in London?"

"Shut the hell up. I've got shit to do."

I stormed out of the room, still furious about the questioning. I couldn't stand that they were talking about her. But maybe the real reason was because I didn't understand why I liked her so much either.

I sped off to the docks. I needed to fuck some shit up and the fuckers in the dungeon would help with that. I wouldn't mind beating the crap out of Jeremiah O'Brien right now.

As I pulled up, I saw Jye was already there. He was standing with Jakob and it looked like they were in a heated discussion.

Could this day get any worse?

I got out of the car and headed over to them, knowing I was going to lose my shit.

"What is it?"

"Ronan O'Brien escaped half an hour ago, I sent the boys out to look for him, but no one has eyes on him yet."

"He fall in the water?" I asked.

"No, he ran for the road."

"Just fucking perfect," I swore. "Remind me why you work for me, Jakob."

Jye pushed Jakob toward the container we were keeping them in as I tried to figure out what to do.

I needed a fucking stiff drink.

TEEGHAN

SLOANE WAS ALREADY FED up with the club tonight. It had taken almost a day and a half of begging her to come out again after the shooting. Obviously, it hadn't put others off. The club was packed. She was drinking heavily and ignoring me for most of it. I could tell she was still upset that I had slept with Conor again.

"Come on, Sloane. Can't we just party and forget all the shit that's happened in this past week?" I asked her. She looked at me, and finally the tough girl faded, her eyes showed me she wanted to have fun. I'd had a tough week. Conor hadn't come to see me, and I hadn't heard from him. Somehow, I hadn't gotten drunk enough to drunk dial him. Thank fuck. It was time to go back to London and to my old life.

"Let's go," I said, taking her hand and leading her to the dance floor. We danced to the music, letting men grind up on us all the while knowing we would never hook up with them. Sloane was laughing, enjoying herself, as if she didn't have a care in the world. That's exactly what she needed.

I was going to miss her crazy attitude, and her sharp wit. She hated London so I doubted she would visit me, and I probably wouldn't visit Ireland again until I had to.

The thought of not having a random, passionate night with Conor again did funny things to my chest. It was like someone was sitting on it, making it hard to breathe.

I made the signal for a drink and she nodded, letting me go to the bar while she danced her worries away. Logan had a drink for me before I hit the bar and I thanked him before taking a deep sip. The cold drink hit my chest and eased the pressure a little.

"Teeghan Kennedy."

I turned my head to see a man standing next to me, in a suit, and a very serious look on his face.

"Come with me."

"Ah hell no," I pushed him away. "Not even likely."

"Tee," Logan said, leaning over the bar. "He works for the O'Farrell's, you best go with him."

I looked up and saw movement on the balcony. They hadn't been here earlier which was why Sloane allowed us to stay. I looked over at the dancefloor, but she was so busy she hadn't noticed. Conor must have wanted to see me, excitement shot through me at the chance to see him again.

"Fine."

He led me to the side stairs which led up to the balcony area. He held the door open to the room which led out onto the balcony. It was usually full of people, but there was no one in this room. In fact, Conor was nowhere to be seen. When Killian turned around and looked through me like I was expendable, I tried to run but his bodyguard caught me and threw me into the room. I could feel the real fear take over then. Killian ushered me over to the balcony. I sat down on a chair, and he sat opposite me.

"Teeghan."

"Yes?"

"What is going on with you and my brother?" he asked me, relaxing into his chair. He had the first five buttons of his shirt undone, and I could see the same tattoo that Conor had on his chest.

"I don't know what you're talking about."

"Cut the crap, Teeghan."

"So, we fuck every now and then, it's not a permanent thing. I'm leaving to go back to London."

"Ah yes," he said, as if he didn't believe me. "When is your last day here?"

"I'm leaving on Saturday."

"Three more days here?"

I nodded. He was wondering if he could believe me. Why would he be asking me about Conor. Did Conor like me back?

"Did Conor pull some shit over in London to help you?" he asked me.

"Conor was in London?"

"Cut the crap."

"Seriously, I thought he was in Dublin. He was in London?"

My mind raced as to why he would go to London. I was still unable to find a job there, but I knew someone who could lend me an apartment for a few weeks while I searched. I had to get away from this city. I had to free myself from Ireland, before it sucked me in completely. I needed to get away from Conor.

I wanted him.

More than I had wanted anyone else in my life and it scared the hell out of me. After seeing his ex, and breaking her nose, I'd realized I would never be enough for him. He was always going to go for the next supermodel.

That's what mafia men did.

"You're saying you and he aren't a thing?" he asked me. I could see by his stiff upper lip that he didn't trust me. Killian was dark. I could see the darker eyes penetrating through me. I actually felt cold when he stared into my eyes.

How was it that sweet and sensitive Sloane could fall in love with a man like this? He was the polar opposite of my brother.

"I told you...we slept together a few times and that's it."

"Why is he making stupid decisions then?" he asked me. "You only do that for someone you care for."

"I don't know anything about his life," I burst out. "I'm serious when I say we fuck and that's it. It doesn't even matter, I'm leaving so why am I even up here?"

My heart was racing in my chest, at first I thought it may be the music pounding loudly throughout the club, but it was my heart trying to rip through my ribcage and flee.

"So you say," he replied. "How do I know you're not trying to manipulate him?"

I rolled my eyes. "Because it's always women who do the manipulating right?"

I stood up, much to the anger of him. His eyes changed instantly. I could feel the anger washing off him in waves. He stood too, but before I could stop myself, I started to walk away. I felt fingers grab my elbow and wheel me around. I was slammed up against the wall, a gun pointed at my temple. My body was shaking in fear, screams wouldn't be heard over the music, but I doubted I could form one in my condition. Killian looked terrifying. He would not hesitate to kill me and get rid of me.

I knew that.

Just from the way he was looking at me, I could tell he would destroy me and throw me into the bay to get rid of me.

Out of the corner of my eyes I saw someone coming up toward us. It wasn't until the gun was off my temple that I saw Killian on the ground, and Conor was on top of him, punching the absolute shit out of him. Blood splattered everywhere around them. The pure rage in Conor frightened me.

I'd never known Conor to be anything but sweet. This couldn't be the same man who wrapped a towel around me after our amazing shower a week ago. The same man who kissed me with fiery intensity until I felt like I was going to burst.

I ran away, as Killian's guys were trying to pull Conor off him, down the stairs and toward the dancefloor.

"Come on," I told Sloane. "We gotta go."

She must have seen the urgency in my eyes, and she followed me out of the club. I turned to make sure no one was following us before I turned to her and said, "You were right, Sloane. The O'Farrell's are monsters."

She pulled me into her arms and gave me a hug I didn't know I needed. "What happened?"

"I can't right now, let's just get out of here before I don't make it out of Ireland again."

Sloane and I took off down the street and toward her apartment.

CHAPTER EIGHT

CONOR

Jye and I sat down on the couch in the apartment we had given to Emma. She'd not even tried to leave yet, probably trying to prove herself to us but I didn't care anymore. If she wanted to run to the police in Ireland, she'd just get delivered back to us and England had no jurisdiction over us. I looked down at my phone but no messages or calls had come through. Jye had told me he gave my number to Teeghan but she'd not once used it.

It was driving me crazy that she wasn't trying to get my attention. Surely, she would know I was back. I saved her from my brother's wrath.

Fuck.

I almost killed him. If it hadn't been for his men pulling me off, I would have killed him. The fucker almost killed Teeghan. He had the nerve to put a fucking gun against Teeghan's head, and to scare her. I didn't care that it hadn't been loaded. He had fucking done it in the first place which had pissed me off to no end.

"Still no word, huh?"

"She hasn't been at her apartment either," I said. "I don't get it."

"I mean...what Killian did to her probably scared the fuck out of her."

Emma walked out of her bathroom and sat down by the window, looking out at the street below.

"Has she spoken to you?"

"A little," he said.

I got up and felt the need to pace. I didn't know what to do. Ronan was still missing, Jeremiah wasn't speaking, Teeghan now wasn't talking to me and I was pretty sure she was leaving tomorrow. How the hell did I get my life so fucking messed up?

My phone dinged and I eagerly pulled it out only to see a name I didn't want to see.

"Why the fuck is Makenna blowing up my phone the last couple of days?" I asked him.

Jye smirked at me. "Oh yeah, I forgot to tell you. Teeghan and Makenna had a bit of an issue with each other at the gym."

"What?"

"Yeah turns out Teeghan can hold her own."

I felt the smile on my face. The thought of Teeghan coming out on top of the queen bee Makenna made me happy.

"So what's this about a nose?"

"She broke Makenna's nose," Jye said, proudly. "But it was caused by Makenna's usual bitchiness but also by the fuckers in the gym kicking her out because of her association with you."

My smile was gone. I felt the anger rise again.

"They kicked her out? Don't we own the gym?"

"We do now," he said. "And the staff were fired."

Good.

No wonder she was pissed at me.

"She hasn't called you, has she?" Emma said, looking over at me.

"How do you know that?"

"It's a small apartment," she replied. "Something you need to know about Teeghan is she's super independent. She doesn't trust easily. So if she's being treated like shit by people because of their fear for you, you need to show her that she's not just a side piece. She's part of a relationship. The reason why she and Andrew didn't work was she didn't conform to what he wanted whereas I did."

"So, what are you saying?"

"She is being treated like a side piece, right?" she asked.

"I suppose she is."

"Well, show her she's more. Keep her in Ireland by showing her what she can do for you, what she is to you. Maintain an open communication. Prove to her that she is worthy of your time and effort. Don't be romantic, she doesn't like that. Be bold, and show her that you trust her."

"Well she leaves for London tomorrow so I doubt I can do that in a day."

Emma bit the inside of her cheek as if she were holding back something she didn't want to spill.

"What?"

"Well, she may want to move back but she won't be able to."

"Why is that?"

"When they got divorced, she kept delaying the proceedings. He thought it was because of her love for him and that excited him but when he realized it was because she had no money, he got mad. He had her blacklisted with every hiring agency in London."

I knew what she told me should have angered me but it actually filled me with hope.

"But she's still going."

"She'll find out sooner or later," she said. "I can try and get it lifted but she wouldn't be having any luck getting an actual job."

I turned to Jye. He had the same look on his face that I imagined was on mine.

Victory.

Now, I just had to get her to see that staying in Ireland was the best for her.

"I can see you think you've won already but she still hasn't contacted you. Teeghan is smart, like really smart. If you don't win her over, she will disappear on you."

"What do I do then?" I asked her.

"Give her something to do, something that she can own like a job or something and then she will have a reason to stay."

Emma made absolute sense. She had no reason to stay. Her father's business wasn't enough, I knew the money was tight in that shop. She needed something more.

And I knew exactly what I needed to do.

TEEGHAN

...JUST THOUGHT YOU SHOULD KNOW. I wish I could help more.

The last line of the email had my anger flaring. My entire opportunity in London was gone. Well from what I read, it was probably never there to begin with. I was black-listed in London.

I looked around my apartment, filled with boxes of my stuff ready to be shipped and now I had nowhere to ship it. Tears began to fill my eyes and I swiped them away before they could fall down over my cheeks. I'd done my best to avoid Conor. Somehow, I knew he could help me. I knew he could get me a job in London if I really wanted it but would he do it?

No. Conor wouldn't help me. He wanted me to stay. The interaction at the club with his brother told me that.

But there was someone who wanted me gone.

Killian.

I grabbed my keys and headed down to my car. As I drove to the nightclub, I didn't expect it to be open. After all, it was a nightclub but I had to try something to get this frustration out. I opened the doors and surprisingly they shifted and opened. I took one step in, knowing this was stupid. Killian tried to kill me last time before Conor had saved me.

"We're closed," I heard his booming voice from somewhere in the darkened room. The skylight gave a little light in the room but all the booths were cloaked in darkness. The light of a laptop screen highlighted someone sitting in one of the booths. My fear rocketed up my spine and I felt bile rise in my throat.

This was a mistake.

"Why are you here?" he asked me, pushing out of the booth and turning on dim lights around the center of the club. It was so much bigger with everyone out of it. Killian's face was full of bruises and little cuts from Conor's beating. It looked incredibly painful.

"I'm sorry to come here unannounced."

"Why are you here?" he repeated, more menacing this time.

"I need your help."

"My help?" he repeated after me. "Why would you think I would ever help you?"

"Because you want your brother back to the way he was, and I need to leave but I don't think he's letting me."

Killian's intensity lowered a little. It was almost like he knew I wasn't putting him on.

"What do you need?"

"I have been blacklisted in London, I can't get a job. I need you to get him to lift it."

Killian frowned. "We don't have any jurisdiction in London, Teeghan. He wouldn't know the first thing to do with blacklisting."

I felt my justified anger slip away. "Really?"

"Yeah," he said. "It wasn't him but if you really want to get free of Ireland, I can help you. We may not have contacts in London but we do in Scotland and Wales. I can help you find a place in either of those countries."

My fierce resolve was disappearing quickly as I stood in front of the monster I knew Killian to be.

"Well?"

"Scotland, I suppose."

He nodded. "I'll get you something next week."

"Next week?" I repeated. "No, I need to leave tomorrow."

"Why?"

"I don't want him to convince me to stay."

I felt everything in me relax after I admitted that. If he had come to my apartment just one more time, I knew I would stay. I would stay for him.

But then I'd say goodbye to who I was because Conor

wouldn't want a woman who wanted things her own way. He would want a woman who just sat down and shut up.

Just like Andrew.

"I can't do it by tomorrow," he told me. "But you can stay at the estate. He's never there and if he does come, he won't go past the dining room."

There was no way in hell I would trust to stay in a place where the O'Farrell's conducted business.

"No. I'll stay with Sloane."

The name alone made his features change. The monster slipped away for a moment, and I saw the longing look in his eyes.

He wasn't over Sloane.

"That's good. Does he know where she lives?"

I shook my head.

"Good. Stay there and I'll send you word when I have something available."

I nodded and left the club before he changed back into the monster I knew he could be. Things changed when I realized it hadn't been Conor who had blacklisted me in London. He probably would let me leave.

Maybe...just maybe I needed to give him the benefit of the doubt. I drove to the shops to get something to bring to Sloane's.

Never turn up without a bottle of wine as she always said. In our case, it wasn't wine, but hard liquor or even enough alcohol to make our own cocktail concoctions.

As I pulled up outside the shops, I looked across the street to see Jye getting out of his car and heading up the stairs to an apartment above a barbershop. I looked up at the window and saw someone I never expected to see again.

Oh hell no.

I marched across the street, my emotions very much in

charge as I took the steps two at a time. I got to the apartment door and knocked.

There was silence until finally after another round of fist pumping on the door, Jye opened the door.

"Hey Teeghan."

I pushed him back and walked into the apartment, looking everywhere for her. I knew I saw her on the street. I wasn't going crazy.

"Where is she?"

"Who?" he asked, playing dumb.

"Don't," I warned him. "I know I saw her in the window."

Out of the corner of my eye, I saw movement. I turned to see her coming out of a room, her hands up in the air. "I'm here, Tee."

"You don't get to call me that," I spat at her. "Why are you here in my town?"

"It's a long story," she said. "But Jye here is helping me."

"Why? You love London."

"I did when I loved Andrew," she said. "But that's over."

"Shocking," I said, sarcastically. "Why the change of heart and how the hell do you know Jye?"

She was shifting her weight to the other foot. Her telltale sign she was going to lie to me. She did it when I confronted her about Andrew the first time and she was doing it now.

I didn't wait for the lie. Instead, I launched myself across the room and tackled her to the ground. She shrieked as I laid slaps and punches on her. I was vaguely aware of being lifted off her with ease. I couldn't take my eyes off the bitch as I was carried into a separate room and the door closed on her as Jye knelt to help her.

I spun around to see Conor looking at me, his dark eyes

barreling into mine. I didn't expect to see him again. I was hoping I didn't but here he was. I'd walked right back here. This was my fault.

Now I stood here, smelling that goddamn cologne that haunted my dreams and seeing that little curl his hair did over his forehead and that smokey look he was giving me had me having to hold off doing what I desperately wanted to do.

"I can explain, Teeghan."

"Really? Do you know what that woman did to me?"

"I do," he admitted. "She's sorry."

"Oh," I backed up. "Is she?"

"Look, Teeghan, you have every right to be mad, but she needed to get out of London."

"Why?"

"Never mind that. Did you know what your ex did to you? He blacklisted you from getting a job in London."

I felt the air leaving my lungs quickly as I stumbled back. I'd blamed the wrong guy. It made more sense that he would do it though. Andrew wanted what he wanted and when he couldn't control you, he lost his shit.

"I can't do this with you."

I made a move to leave but he grabbed my elbow and pulled me back. I pulled my arm from his hand angrily.

"Don't fucking touch me."

He backed up, looking pained. It looked like it hurt him to hear me say that. That couldn't be true though. Why the fuck would he care?

"Sorry for breaking your girlfriend's nose by the way," I said. "She's kind of a bitch though."

"Makenna is a girl I was with for all of two months," he said, that annoying little smirk on his mouth I desperately wanted to slap off. "She's not my girl."

"Well, I'm sure you'll find another just like her when I'm gone."

I made a move to leave again but he grabbed me and walked me backward. "You aren't leaving Ireland."

It wasn't a question, or a request, it was a demand. He was telling me. Fear pulsed through me as I looked into his dark eyes. My skin pimpled with goosebumps as I felt his warm body against mine.

His mouth claimed mine in a heated kiss. I was lost in his arms as I returned the kiss, wrapping my arms around his neck and allowing him to lead me to the wall. It felt so good to be in his arms again, so good for him to be kissing me into another dimension. How could I say goodbye to this?

But I had to.

He'd never be loyal.

Never be a one woman man.

I'd end up having my heart crushed into pieces.

I pushed him away and ducked under his arm to get to the door. With my hand on the knob, I felt confident enough to turn back to him.

"If she's here, you did something to her lover boy."

"I killed him."

I don't know what I expected him to say but that surprised me. A flood of emotions flit through my entire body. I didn't know how to process it.

"I'm leaving Ireland and you have nothing that will keep me here," I told him. "You once called me Merida. Well just like Merida, I'm choosing me."

"You're not leaving," he said, resolute. The hard criminal that he was standing there, every inch the monster I originally knew him to be.

"Watch me."

With that, I turned the doorknob and walked out of the room and out of the apartment before I ran back into his arms forever.

CONOR

JYE HELD the door open and I entered the church. It was dark as usual, with the altar of candles giving off all the light needed in the room. Murphy was at the confessional, looking down at something in his hand. When we started walking down the aisle, he looked up, a warm smile on his face.

"Has it come?" he asked, eagerly.

"It has," I replied. "First, we need an answer to a question before we can hand it over."

This smile dropped instantly. He knew. You didn't survive in such a powerful position in Galway unless you knew things. Murphy was no saint, after all, he had been friends with my father since school days.

"And what would that question be?" he asked with a hardened tone.

"You know what I'm going to ask so why make it so difficult?" I enquired as I took a seat in front of him, on the corner of the first pew. Jye stood, leaning against the other pew, opposite me so that he was cornered.

Murphy stood his ground, possibly thinking about what he could do to get out of betraying the O'Brien's.

"Are you one of them, Murph?" Jye asked.

Murphy was outraged, which was answer enough. "No."

"Who is it?" I asked him. "Who am I going after?"

"You know I can't speak about such things."

"What would my father say if he knew you had this secret that could destroy his legacy?" I asked him, playing on his memory of my father.

"You destroyed it," he spat back. "It should have gone directly to Lorcan and Killian should have been the second in charge. It should never have been split."

Finally, the true Murphy comes to play. I looked at the man who had helped me when my father had kicked me out of the house. The man who had sheltered me, who had fed me when I needed it. The one who taught me there was no better thing in life than family.

He seemed to realize that I knew I had rattled him, and he straightened his back and took on a calm stance yet again.

"I'll be by to collect the contents of my container tomorrow."

"Are you sure you want to leave the *contents* inside that long?" Jye asked, a smirk on his face.

Murphy turned to him quickly. "You promised not to look inside."

"No," Jye corrected. "Conor promised he wouldn't, I made no such promise. It'd be a stupid business decision to allow a container to arrive in town and not know the contents."

Murphy was furious. His eyes were dark, his lips were tight, a thin white line showing just how angry he was.

"Well, Murphy, looks like you shipped something to us that may be illegal."

He shot a look at me which should have scared me, but I could feel he was unraveling. He couldn't talk his way out of this once. If Jye knew we had something over him, then it was something bad.

I was curious.

But I had made a promise to a man of the cloth, and I took that seriously.

"What do you need to know?" he asked, defeated. "I'll answer one question and that is all so think carefully."

I looked to Jye, who thought the secret was good enough that I could get more. Jye and I had been good mates since school. He would never betray me, and I would never betray him. We could also read each other just with a look.

"Who is it?" I asked him.

"It was started by the O'Brien's," he told me. "But it is not what you think, this feud was started a long, long time ago and one that Paul recently heard about. It ignited an anger in him he had tried to bury with your father."

"What feud?" I asked him.

"I said one question."

"Trust me, Father, you don't want your little secret getting out," Jye said. Murphy battled against his own rage.

"Your grandfather had ruined an O'Brien girl, he had kidnapped her, held her hostage, knowing full well the ransom couldn't be paid. When she was finally set free, she was pregnant and claiming rape."

"So this was my grandfather...he raped a girl, it's probably not the worst thing he did. He was a fucking monster."

"I remember," Murphy said. "But on her deathbed, the girl admitted he never raped her. She had fallen for him, but he refused to leave his wife and she wanted to hurt him."

"So, problem solved."

"No, the girl ended up killing herself," Murphy said. "Making the brother of the girl hellbent on ending your grandfather. He failed, instead, killing your grandmother by mistake."

I'd heard my grandmother had been killed but no one ever said how. I had always assumed it had been a car accident, but being the wife of an O'Farrell was dangerous business. It would make more sense she had become collateral damage.

"So, this started the rebellion?" I asked. "I don't understand why we're getting a history lesson."

"It started because Paul O'Brien has always hated your father," Murphy said. "When he discovered the true history of what happened, he decided to take the anger about it on himself. He wants to see the end of the O'Farrell's and he's using this as a catalyst."

"Paul couldn't pull something this sophisticated," Jye said.

"Ronan could," Murphy said. "Ronan is the brains, Paul is the face of it but only because everyone knows him."

Ronan fucking O'Brien, who conveniently just escaped from us. Well, we still had Jeremiah and he was no way near as intelligent as his brother. He'd crack with minimal torture but he would also be able to tell me everything because Ronan was loyal to his family and he fought daily to keep his brother in the business.

He'd been a protector to him in school too which meant he would try and rescue him soon. I had to be ready.

"Thanks, Murph."

I stood up and Jye and I headed out when Murphy called out to us, "Maybe it's best you dump the container in the ocean."

Jye began to chuckle. "Brutal."

"OK, I gotta know what it is now."

"Seems like the container belongs to us now, we'll open it up and I'll show you exactly what the good Father is into."

I couldn't help but laugh as we got in Jye's car and took off back to the docks. Whatever it was, it was bad considering how Murphy acted and then to be so callous as to want it destroyed.

Something inside of me already knew what it was and it was definitely something we could use if needed.

I CHECKED the clock in my car and drove down the driveway of the estate. I was late.

Again.

These last-minute requests for family meetings were starting to take a toll. Before Teeghan, we rarely saw each other and now it was almost every second day.

Teeghan.

Probably the reason for the last minute request for a meeting too. She seemed to be the only one they wanted to talk about which annoyed the fuck out of me. Why couldn't they get over the fact that I had a woman?

A woman who didn't want a bar of me since she found out I had killed her ex. I had destroyed so much furniture in that apartment after she left that Jye had to stop me. He even took Emma out of the apartment and put her up in another safe house we had.

Fuck.

I didn't know how to handle the feelings I had for her so I went back to work. I did what I had to put her at the back of my mind. She was determined to leave. She didn't want me as much as I wanted her, so the gentlemanly thing would be to let her leave, right?

I could find another woman. I could find someone tomorrow to satisfy my needs, but I knew none would shine in comparison to my Merida.

As I made my way inside, Walter took my jacket and I headed into the dining room. Lorcan sat at the head of the table as always, and Killian sat on the side next to him. His face was still bruised and cut from my attack on him which made me smile. He noticed and rolled his eyes, flicking the middle finger up at me. I pulled the seat out at the end of the table and sat down. Walter put a whiskey down in front of me and left the room. I could hear the storm beginning to rumble outside. It was meant to really bucket down tonight. I wanted to get out of here before that happened. The very thought of being stuck here for god knew how long didn't really feel like something I wanted to go through.

"Well?" I cracked, my anger taking all of my patience with it.

"We're worried about you. It's not like you to be infatuated with a woman," Lorcan said.

"Why did you go to London?" Killian asked me.

The bruises and cuts on his face from my attack looked like they were giving him great pain. I couldn't even try to feel sorry for him. He shouldn't have touched her.

I shrugged my shoulders which only angered Lorcan. I could see his already thin patience running even thinner. His fists were balling on top of the table and he looked over at me.

"You're losing your edge," he told me. "It's not like you to be so balled up over a woman."

"How so?" I countered, knowing full well what they were trying to insinuate. I just didn't want to talk about it.

Lorcan slammed his hands down on the table and stood, his arms still on the top of the table surface.

"We are helping her to get a job so she can get away from your obsession with her," he said.

I could feel my rage start to rear its ugly head again. "If you do that, or try to go near Teeghan, I will kill you."

I pushed up off the chair. They looked at me like I was crazy, Lorcan's anger written all over his face told me that I may have to put hands on him. He was the only one who wasn't scared of my anger. I needed to get out of here before I acted on my threat.

Pushing the chair so that it fell backward, I stepped around it and headed for the door. Opening the large door, I looked out at the storm raging. Rain poured from the sky and lighting was seen not too far off in the distance.

Shit.

"Con," Walter came running up to me. "Please, wait out this storm. It's not safe, I've heard the storm has knocked the lights out in the city center."

As if on cue, the lights in the house went out.

Fuck.

I heard Lorcan barking orders for people to try and get the lights back on and they all scattered throughout the house.

"Fine," I said, slamming the door shut. "But only until it stops then I'm out."

He nodded to me and I headed upstairs to my room. Surely it wouldn't last all night.

TEEGHAN

I LOOKED at the tiny bit of vodka left in the bottom of the bottle and then at Sloane who was laughing her head off.

"It wasn't a full bottle, so relax," she said, chuckling as she got up. "I've got another bottle somewhere in here."

"God, if we drink a bottle of vodka a night, I may not need to move to Scotland, I'll be dead."

Sloane rolled her eyes and poured another drink for me and then topped up hers before we sat back down on the bean bags, looking out at the night sky through her sliding doors to her balcony. It was raining heavily so we couldn't sit out there even though it was the best part of her shoebox apartment.

"So," she said finally. "Scotland, hey."

"Yeah, London is a no go apparently."

"Because of Andrew?"

I nodded. Thoughts of what I'd learned yesterday had me feeling emotional again. I wasn't as emotional as I thought I would be.

"Are you sure he's dead?" she asked me.

"He told me he killed him," I replied. "I don't think he makes light of who he kills."

"That's true. The family have never shied away from killing when they want to."

"I just...I don't feel like crying about it," I said, admitting I was at odds with how to feel. "Isn't that weird?"

Sloane sighed. "Teeghan, you were never in love with him. You married him to be free of Ireland. You never liked it here."

"That's not entirely true," I told her. I'd never really opened up about why I truly left, not to anyone. "I left because I had no prospects here. No one wanted to have anything to do with me after the thing with Evie."

Sloane sat up. "Oh my god, I forgot about that."

"It wasn't my finest moment."

Reliving the memory of what I did to that poor girl wasn't something I wanted to deal with. My emotions had been at the forefront when I was 15. I didn't mean to go as far as I did but she'd been mortified when I'd been finished with her.

I didn't like who I had been back then.

"What ever happened to her?" Sloane asked me.

"You live here, you tell me," I chuckled.

"I don't think I've seen her in years," she said.

"She must have gotten out," I told her. "This town can suck you down sometimes."

Sloane nodded. "I hear that."

"Why didn't you ever leave?" I asked her. "I mean after Sean."

"Honestly," she said, turning to look at me. "I never wanted to."

I looked out at the storm again and wondered what would happen if I were to stay. Enough time had passed that no one could still blame me for my attack on Evie. The one that almost sent me to juvenile detention.

"Do you wonder why Conor killed Andrew?" Sloane asked me after a few minutes of silence.

"It's what he does, isn't it?" I spoke. "Isn't that his way of showing me he wants me?"

"I think it's more than that," Sloane said. "Look, as much as they are monsters and all that. I know for a fact that the O'Farrell's only kill to stay on top but they only do it when they can't see any way out of it. Conor is one of the kindest of the brothers. I think that he did it because Andrew was talking about you in a less than honorable way."

That didn't surprise me. Andrew had a foul mouth on him and had no problem in making you feel ant size when he wanted you to hurt.

If that were the case and Conor had defended my honor by silencing him, maybe I did have to say thank you. Maybe

I did owe him a chance to tell me why he went there and why he's harboring Emma, the backstabber.

I was getting up to get another drink when I heard her door handle jiggle. I turned just as she jumped up and we both watched as the locked door knob jiggled violently before the door burst open.

We looked at the masked men who came inside, directly for me. Sloane screamed at them to leave but they paid her no attention. I froze on the spot. It didn't matter that I knew how to defend myself, well I knew some moves. Rather than running like Sloane was screaming at me to do, I stood still on the spot and looked at the fierce eyes through the balaclava as they came for me. Sloane was battling one of them who was trying to grab her.

Something in seeing my best friend being attacked sparked something in me. I poked my fingers into my aggressor's eyes. He backed up, blinded momentarily before I ran for Sloane. I jumped on the guy's back so she could run. She ran for her phone and dialed someone.

I assumed it was the police as she hung up just as quickly and came to help me. My arms were getting tired. Just as I thought the guy was going to go down, I felt myself being lifted off his back and suddenly I felt something hard come down on my head before my vision blurred and everything went black.

CHAPTER NINE

CONOR

I could see the pools of water in the gardens under my window. This storm had been raging for hours now. My phone had no reception and the house line had been disconnected years ago. I sat on my windowsill, watching the choppy waves crash against each other before they crashed onto the shore. The door to my room was pushed open and I saw Killian looking more worried than I had ever seen him in my life.

"Get up and come with me," he said, urgently. I knew better than to argue when he was in this way. I followed him blindly down the hall and toward the garage.

"Where are we going?" I asked.

He didn't respond. Instead, he got in the car and I jumped in beside him. He took off down the driveway of the estate and into the city. His hand was fidgeting and I could see he was freaking out internally.

"Fuck Killian, just spill it."

"Something happened at Sloane's," he said, turning to

me quickly before going back to the road. "She said someone took Teeghan."

My heartbeat faster and my stomach dropped. This was my fault. They took her because of me.

"Who?"

"We're going to Sloane's so she can tell us everything. She called me mid attack but she texted right after and said they took Teeghan and left."

"Why'd she call you?" I asked.

"She knows I will actually do something about it," he said. "She trusts me. Just leave it at that."

I knew not to push him anymore. Killian and I were similar in that aspect. Someone went after someone I love, I would do anything to protect that person. He was the same, only he relished the hunt. It was more of a task for me. Killian sped through the rain-soaked streets until we pulled up outside of an apartment block just outside the city. We ran into the building and up the stairs to the second floor. The door was slightly ajar, and Sloane was holding something on top of her head as we entered.

She'd been crying, and had obviously copped a bit of a beating. She began to sob as Killian entered the apartment. He took her into his arms quickly. I looked at the nasty cut on her forehead that she'd been applying an ice brick to.

"Who were they?" I asked her, my heart still hadn't returned to its original beat.

"I don't know," she said, pulling from Killian's arms. I could see he was concerned as he looked at her wounds. She applied the ice back to her head. "They had balaclavas on. I didn't even hear them speak. They just came in and ambushed us. She tried to help me and that's when I broke away to call you but then they grabbed her before I could get to the kitchen for a knife. I came back and there was one left. He looked at me, and I swear, Kill, he looked so evil. I just saw those dark eyes and I thought I was going to shit myself. He hit me over the head, and I fell. Then he kicked me. I just remember him leaving and then I got up to call you again."

"Was there anything you recognized about them?" Killian asked.

"No," she said, irritated. "I don't tend to spend much time with evil mercenaries."

"I know this is hard," he said. "I just need to find a way to find them to help Teeghan."

Something in her shifted and it looked like she remembered something.

"Oh," she said. "When they hit her over the head. She looked up at the guy and she must have recognized him. She said a name, like she knew him, and she was surprised he had hurt her."

"What was the name?" I asked her, coming to stand in front of her.

"I don't know, I didn't hear it," she said. "I just saw the way she looked up at him. She was really surprised."

"Who does she know really well in town?" Killian asked.

"Honestly, I don't know. She doesn't tend to make friends too easy."

I'd been hearing that a lot lately and it only made me want her more. I was the same, in every way. Never trusting, always just keeping everyone at arm's length. Maybe that's why I couldn't stay away from her.

She was a kindred spirit or whatever the fuck it was.

"Ask her father, he may know."

I was doubtful. He wanted me to stay away from her

and now I had to go and tell him she had been taken because of me.

A slight knock on the door had Killian and I drawing our guns and aiming it at the police officer at the door. He had one hand on his gun on his hip before he threw his hands up.

"I'm sorry. I was alerted to an incident here by a neighbor. Is everyone all right?" he asked.

"Sorry, Officer, they were leaving. You can come in."

He did, taking a notebook out of his pocket and a pencil. Killian and I started to head out as Sloane headed to the cop. She grabbed Killian's hand as he was passing which stopped us.

She looked from the cop to Killian. "Evil eyes."

We both looked at the cop who drew his gun to shoot Sloane and then us. I was faster, taking his hand out with a bullet before he got a shot off. He dropped the gun and fell to the floor, cradling his bleeding hand.

"Sloane, you don't want to see this. Go to the estate. We'll keep you safe until we get this shit sorted."

She didn't hesitate. She grabbed her phone and keys and headed out of the apartment.

"I assume you have a place for this piece of shit while I fill Lorcan in."

"You know it."

Killian left me with the cop, and I grabbed my phone to dial Jye. We had a perfect place to string him up and get answers.

TEEGHAN

I SQUEEZED my eyes shut tight, the pain making my brain swim around in my skull. My mouth was dry, making it hard to swallow and my entire body felt like it was stiff. Slowly, I opened my eyes, dodging the brightness from the window, and looking around. I was on an uncomfortable bed, in a completely foreign room. I put my hand up to my head, but it hurt when I touched it. I sat up, hearing a clanging noise from behind me. I looked down at my right hand, it was handcuffed to the steel bedpost. I tried to pull it closer to me but the post held it straight. I tried squeezing the cuff off my hand by shoving my thumb in the middle of my palm but it wouldn't budge. I only caused my hands to hurt with the action.

Where the hell was I?

I tried to think back to the last thing I could remember. That's when I remembered. I saw his eyes and immediately I knew who he was. When I had said his name, he'd clocked me again and I just remembered seeing black until now.

Ronan.

We'd been friends growing up but had parted ways as we got older and I was more determined than ever to leave Ireland for a better life.

"Ronan," I called out. I saw the door in front of me, it was a cheap little wooden thing that would be easy to hear through. It took a few more calls before the door opened and I saw Ronan standing there, flustered. His usual white, clammy cheeks were red and he looked utterly mortified.

"How could you have known it was me?" he asked me. "I had a mask on."

"I know your eyes, dummy," I said. "Unchain me."

"I can't do that," he said, closing the door behind him and coming to sit on the bed in front of me. "Look, I didn't think you'd get caught up with an O'Farrell, but since you did, we need to hold you here. It's more for your safety too, you know."

"If it were for my safety, you wouldn't have chained me up. I leave in a week, Ronan. A fucking week and I'll be gone."

He looked sad, like he wasn't the one in charge here. I knew exactly why I was here. I was fuel for a war with Conor.

Inside, I was raging. These motherfuckers thought they could outwit the O'Farrell's. I knew he'd come for me. I knew he would, but I didn't want him to die with thoughts of saving me.

I wanted him to kill them all.

In fact, I wanted to kill them all myself.

"Conor is going to fucking kill you."

"No he won't," he said with a sigh. "He has my brother. We just want him back."

"That's not what you want," I replied. "And you'll never give me back to him. You want total devastation and you only achieve that with my death."

He didn't respond immediately and my fears were realized. I wasn't making it off his bed. I'd never see Sloane, my dad or Conor again. My chest began to rise and fall rapidly, staving off the sobs that would come when he left.

I didn't want him to see me weak. No one would see me weak, ever again. I'd sworn that to myself when I signed the papers to Andrew.

"Tee, please, just be quiet and I'll get this sorted. You don't need to get hurt."

I hocked my spit at him. It landed just under his eye. He got up and wiped it away with the sleeve of his shirt before he looked down at me.

"Please don't be your usual self," he begged. "It's not

just me here, watching you and these guys can do brutal things to women."

I knew he said it to scare me, but I knew if they came even an iota of being within my reach I would crush them.

Big talk for someone who froze when they came for her. If I hadn't frozen, I would have easily been able to grab a weapon and get them gone. Then I'd have the O'Farrell's protecting me.

If only.

Ronan left the room, once the door closed and I heard the lock click from the outside, I tried everything I could to get the cuff off me but to no avail. My wrist was red raw and my entire hand ached. I tried to look around the room for anything I could use to help me, but the room was as bare as a prison cell. I could see a window to the side of the room and as I looked out at the bay, I realized we were on the other side of the bay, in the forest that no one trekked through due to the thickness of the bush.

I was well and truly fucked.

CHAPTER TEN

CONOR

Jye laid a punch into Jeremiah's stomach again, forcing a strangled groan, toppled with more blood pouring from his mouth. He hadn't given up a damn thing about his brother. Just maybe we had it wrong about Jeremiah. He was always known as the stupid one, but maybe he was the smarter of them both. I had to give him props, he was still awake. We'd been at this for over forty minutes now.

If anything happened in the time it took to find Teeghan, I would personally beat the rest of the life out of him and go after anyone connected to him.

"Where is she?" Jye asked again, cracking his knuckles. I could tell the punching was wearing on Jye too. We weren't going to get very far with this, and where would I be if I lost my most trusted man.

"I don't know," Jeremiah yelled, blood spilling out over his lips and down on his lap. "I've been here, remember. Ronan does what Ronan wants to do."

Jye slapped him across the face and came over to me.

"Best thing we could do is drive around, ask questions."

"I know Murphy knows something," I told him. "Especially with what I know about him now. Did you take care of the contents?"

"Absolutely, and already know we can use it against him if we need to."

"Perfect. I have a feeling he's going to be using something the rebellion can use against us."

"Let's get cleaned up and we'll head into the town to track down some leads."

We locked Jeremiah back up in the dungeon and headed for the office. Cleaning up the blood, we made sure that we didn't have a spot on us as we headed into the city center. Something about this rebellion had my blood boiling and not just because they had taken my woman.

My woman.

I hoped like hell she was giving them shit, the fiery redhead had completely blown me apart on the inside because of her sharp wit the first time we met. I got in the passenger seat of the car and Jye took the driver's seat. I couldn't contain my anger anymore, I was going to burst. I slammed my fist against the car door and slid down in my seat.

Jye didn't even try to look over at me.

"We'll get her back, they wouldn't be stupid enough to hurt her."

Out of everyone, Jye was the only one who hadn't had something to say about her. He never did speak his mind unless we were blind drunk or I asked him what he thought. If he could accept her, why couldn't my own brothers?

Then again, I'd never wanted her to be subject to this life, I never wanted any woman to be, which was why I lived my life the way I did. It wasn't exactly easy on women.

My mother had hated it, but she'd loved my father, and so she put up with the cheating, the mistresses, the scandals, the rumors and she raised us to the best of her ability before she died.

I knew one thing for sure.

Teeghan was never, ever going to feel like that. I was done with other women. She was it for me. I could feel it that very first night, and that was why it had unsettled me. I'd tried to stay away from her, tried to tell myself I would be wrong for her but fuck it, I couldn't stand the idea of her being with someone else.

I didn't want anyone else seeing that body or to see her red curls bouncing around as she rode him for all he was worth.

That was for me.

And me only.

Jye pulled up outside the church and we headed inside. Murphy would have to know what was going on. Surely.

He knew everything.

The bastard.

The candles weren't lit at the altar, and I couldn't hear him in the church anywhere. The confessional was empty and so was his office.

Jye pulled the torch up on his phone and shone it through the abandoned church.

"Where the fuck is he?" Jye asked. "He's never not here."

"Unless he's fucking involved in Teeghan's disappearance," I offered. The very thought made me ball my fists up, ready to punch anyone and anything. I could have taken him out ages ago if I'd known how fucking sick he was.

"Would he really be that stupid?" Jye asked.

I hoped like hell not, but it wasn't like I was on the ball

lately. A certain red haired woman had brought me clear to my knees and she was all I thought about.

"Come on," I said. "I think I know who else we can go to."

As we exited out of the church, I saw Killian leaning against our car. Sloane was with him, and she looked angry.

"What is it?" I asked him.

"What did Murphy say?" he asked me.

"He wasn't there," I said.

Killian frowned, as did Sloane. "But he's always here."

I shrugged. "I don't know what to tell ya."

He looked to Sloane briefly before he turned back to me. "Come on, we should get back to the estate and figure out what the fuck we're going to do."

"Why? You're helping her to flee from me. Why would you want to help me get her back?" I asked, suspicious.

"We can help," he said. "You don't have to go off half-cocked and get yourself killed."

"He's right," Jye said from beside me. I knew he was. He was always fucking right but it didn't mean I wanted to believe he would ever have my best interest at heart. Killian did what Killian wanted to and that was it.

We were about to get in my car. Killian headed to his car with Sloane.

"Maybe Sloane should stay at home," I said to Killian over the top of my car.

"Like hell," she edged out from behind Killian, her hands on her hips. I could see she was just as feisty as Teeghan. "I am coming with you. You got her into this trouble and now I'm going to do what I should have done before and rescue her from you and your family's bullshit."

"Let's just fucking find her first," Jye said, exasperatedly. "Then we can argue and shit."

We piled into our cars and headed back to the estate. Lorcan knew more about the business when our father ran it. He may know who Murphy was closest to and we could crush some skulls for information.

This whole waiting shit was doing nothing for my already limited patience. She was in the enemy's hands. I didn't want to think what they could be doing to her because of me.

If she had a fucking thing wrong with her when we finally got her, I would fucking burn down every goddamn building they owned and kill all of their families.

No one fucked with the O'Farrell's.

And she was one of us.

TEEGHAN

MY WRISTS WERE RED RAW, blood smearing the metal cuffs clamped around my wrists. I could barely feel the pain anymore as I tried to push the steel post off the bed with my feet. The pulling only made the cuffs smash against my wrists more. I had to be careful not to nick a vein in my wrist.

That'd be a pretty stupid way to go.

The door opened and I tried to hide the damage to my wrists. I looked up to see Ronan standing by the doorway with a brown paper bag in one hand and a drink in the other.

"Any whiskey in that?" I asked him, a sickened laugh coming from within me. This wasn't funny. It was humiliating but I felt a little woozy, almost like I was tipsy.

"Sorry, no," he said. "I can get you some if you want."

"Oh, how nice of you," I bit back. "Fuck off."

He put the bag down on the side of the mattress I wasn't on and the drink on the chair over by the door. I looked out of the door, only to see someone I recognized.

Someone that shouldn't be here.

Ronan blocked my view again but I knew that guy was one of Conor's men. I looked back at Ronan, that little pathetic look on his face wasn't fooling me.

"I can't fucking reach that drink, you know."

He looked back over to it and sighed, pulling the chair closer and putting it next to the bed.

"Better?"

"I need at least one hand free, fuckhead."

"If you're not going to be nice to me, I'm not going to be nice back, Tee. This was a courtesy as an old friend."

"Some fucking friend," I replied quickly. "Conor is going to fuck you up when he finds me."

Ronan's sheepish look changed dramatically to one of anger. Raw, unadulterated anger. He really fucking hated Conor.

Which meant the guy who I just saw was a mole, giving the rebellion information on Conor. Instantly I felt protective over the man who had pulled me down into this world.

The man I would fucking kill for.

Shit, Tee, you went and fell in love with the mafia.

Da was going to be pissed.

"Conor couldn't find a whore in a whorehouse," Ronan finally said, angrily.

"You visit them often, Ronan?" I responded. He marched back outside and slammed the door shut, locking it. I felt a little victory going off inside of me at making him so mad. Finally, the real Ronan came to play. Looking down at the brown paper bag, I tried to pull it open but when I looked down at the burger, I realized there was no way in hell I would be able to eat it while handcuffed to the bed.

"Just fucking great, you wanker," I yelled. "How about some fucking food I can eat while handcuffed."

The door swung open and a man I'd never met before looked down at my bloody wrists and the bag. He saw the burger and my hands and shook his head. He left the room only to return and unlock me from the bed. I was still hand-cuffed but now I could move about.

"Don't try anything or I'll put a bullet in your head," he said.

I believed it too.

I nodded and he left the room again and locked it. The smell from the burger was tantalizing, so much so, my stomach growled loudly. I had to risk a possible drugging and eat because there was no way in hell I would get through another day with no food. Everyone says you can live without food for days, but they obviously didn't love food as much as I did.

Fuck the bitches who never ate, and kept a skinny figure, I'd rather my lumps and bumps if it meant binging on cake, pasta and burgers.

The sun was going down, I could see the sunset hitting the water at just the right angle. It was pretty.

Too bad I was handcuffed, in pain, and probably about to be murdered to get back at Conor.

Thinking about that made the food hit my empty stomach hard, burning. It was almost tasteless as I wondered if this mediocre, cold burger would be the last thing I were to eat before I died.

CHAPTER ELEVEN

TEEGHAN

Ronan opened the door again, startling me awake. I sat up, and pulled my hands in front of me, protectively.

"I'm not going to fucking hurt you, Tee."

He closed the door behind him and took a seat on the chair next to the bed. "Conor isn't answering my calls. I want my brother back."

"So?"

"So, I need you to convince him. Leave him a message."

"And say what? Come have some cookies with your enemy, they won't try anything, they've only chained me up to a bed for two days."

Ronan rolled his eyes. "Why do you have to be such a bitch?"

"Oh, I'm sorry, is it inconveniencing you that I'm not cooperating when you kidnapped me and are holding me hostage, handcuffed the entire time?"

Ronan stood up, groaning loudly as he paced the room.

"I need my brother back. They'll keep torturing him if I don't get him and he's not strong enough."

"Are you worried he'll crack like Humpty Dumpty?" I asked, proud of my own joke.

"Teeghan," he said with a warning tone. "Send him a message."

"Fine, give me your damn phone."

He did, dialing the number for me and holding it to my ear so I couldn't secretly send another message without his knowledge. The fucker was smarter than I thought.

The phone rang out and I heard the beep signaling for me to leave a message.

"Conor, Ronan is forcing me to leave you a message to say I'm fine. Please answer the phone when he calls you again or else I'll likely be shot in the head. Don't worry, I'm enjoying my prison, it has quite the view of the bay."

Ronan pulled the phone away from me, his face full of fury. "Are you fucking kidding me?"

"Oh please, it's not like I could give him fucking coordinates."

He was about to turn and leave when I thought of what I could do to help myself. "I need to pee."

He turned around. "Do you really?"

"Hey, you gave me a drink, eventually it needs to come out," I shrugged my shoulders, hopefully pulling off a casual look.

He rolled his eyes and came over to me, hauling me off the bed and out of the room. Everyone stopped talking, including the fucker betraying Conor, and I was shoved into a small room with a toilet.

"Uh, I need to be able to wipe," I said, holding my wrists out. "It's not like women can just shake it off."

Ronan was contemplating it before he sighed and

pulled a key from his pocket and undid one cuff. He kept the other one on me, in order to get them fastened quickly afterward. I closed the door and sat down, forcing myself to pee to make the sound. The room didn't even have a window.

Fuck me. Where the hell were we? I hoped like hell my hint would help Conor. I finished up and opened the door to find Ronan gone and Conor's man standing there, a sick smile on his face.

"Do you know who I am?" he asked me, grabbing my wrist and pulling me back to my room with force.

"I know you got an ugly mug of a face," I said. "I also know you can betray anyone at the drop of a dime."

"Fuck off," he said. "Just because you got a snatch that latched onto Conor and didn't let go, doesn't mean you know nothin'."

He shoved me into the room. I looked back at him, a sick grin on his face as he looked me up and down like I was Sunday afters. My skin prickled with unease as I felt naked under his gaze even though I was heavily dressed.

This was it, Tee. I ran at him, shoving my head down so I could spear him in the middle but all I felt was a heavy thud on the back of my head before I fell hard on the ground. His face hovering over mine as I was rolled over.

His sick grin was the last thing I saw before the darkness took over.

CONOR

JYE LISTENED to the voicemail again. Hearing her sarcastic tone made me smile. Obviously, she was unhurt but if she kept it up with her attitude, she may not be by the time we found her.

"What do you think she meant?" I asked him.

"View of the bay," Jye said. "There aren't many places that she could be with a view unless she were stowed away in a warehouse or an estate. This estate overlooks the bay so she might be close."

"There are no other estates," Killian said, as annoyed as I was. It had been hours since we came here to gather support to split up and look through places we know are protected by the rebellion.

"There is one place," Lorcan said, coming from another room. We hadn't even known he was here. Killian may be on my side with Tee but Lorcan most certainly wasn't. He hadn't been the same since he lost the woman he loved years ago. "The cottage on the other side of the bay. It belongs to the O'Brien's."

"Wasn't it demolished over a decade ago?" Killian asked. "I'm sure da did that."

I walked over to the windows and looked out at the bay, I looked around at the warehouses down by the bay, which led out onto the docks, on the far side, I saw the woods.

"Does anyone have binoculars?" I asked, feeling like an idiot. Did anyone have a pair of binoculars anymore? Lorcan moved out of the room and came back a few minutes later with a pair of them.

"Serious?"

"You asked."

I held them up to the windows and looked back at the woods. That's when I saw it. A small cottage buried in a lot of trees, but right on the water's edge.

Motherfucker.

"It's right on the fucking water," I said, putting the

binoculars back down. "She gave us everything but a fucking key."

"Let's go," Killian said, jumping up, and getting ready. Lorcan grabbed his gun from the side cabinet.

"You're coming?" I asked, surprised.

"She's yours, right?" he replied.

"Yeah."

"Then they attacked one of us," Lorcan said to me. "They attack us, we attack them. Together."

"No one fucks with the O'Farrell's," Killian pronounced before our most trusted men agreed in unison.

We piled into our cars and took off toward the cottage and toward my woman.

⁂

Killian had his men, Liam and Tommy, coming up on the back of the cottage, through the trees. Lorcan and his friend Rian were backing us up in the woods when needed. I had Jye and his cousins Declan and Jimmy backing me up.

"Con," Jye grabbed my arm. "We got your back, go and get her out. We'll take out whoever is inside and meet you back at the estate."

I nodded. We all waited for the time we all agreed on to attack, a blitz on the cottage. They wouldn't get out alive.

No one fucks with the O'Farrell's.

I ran for the front door, Jye was kicking it down with ferocity. The rickety wooden door hinges were sent flying as we entered the small room, men jumping up everywhere in surprise. There weren't as many as I had originally thought and Ronan was nowhere to be seen. I ran for every door, looking for Teeghan. Finally, I came to one that was locked. I shot at the lock, sending the door open with a creak. I saw her covering herself with a chair. I moved into the room, and hauled the chair away.

She was bleeding but she was okay.

I was going to fucking kill Ronan. When she looked up at me, I saw the relief in them which made it all worth it. I'd wage fucking war on all of Ireland for this woman. I pulled her up from the floor, noticing the handcuffs on her bloodied wrists.

Jesus Christ.

I pulled her hands out, so the cuff chain was tight, and I shot through the chain, separating her wrists. Taking her hand, I pulled her behind me and through the house. Bodies lay all around, my men had secured the fucking cottage.

"Ronan ain't here," Jye said. "But look who we found."

I looked behind him and saw someone I never thought I would ever see behind enemy lines. Someone I never imagined would betray me.

Jakob.

He looked terrified, as he should, he knew I would never forgive him for this. The only thing stopping me was Teeghan. I didn't want her to see what I was about to do to him.

"Take him to the d–"

I stopped mid-sentence when Teeghan let go of my hand and I wheeled around to see she had reached down to the ground where a gun had been laying. She took the safety off and marched closer to Jakob. No one dared to move. I watched as she aimed the gun at Jakob's face. He whimpered and sobbed, trying to get away.

"You picked the wrong side," she said, angrily. The shot rang out, and Jakob slumped down on the sofa he had been planted on. Lorcan moved toward her and grabbed the gun. She turned around and looked at me.

"Can we get something to eat, I'm starving."

I couldn't help the relieved laugh that erupted out of me. I took her hand and headed out the doorway and to the car. Jye could get a ride back with the others.

I was taking Teeghan to the estate and I was going to show her exactly what we were about and how much she meant to me.

She was mine.

And everyone needed to know you didn't fuck with my woman.

TEEGHAN

When Conor stopped the car, I looked out at the grand estate I had heard about but never seen the inside of. This place was seen from pretty much everywhere in town, either fully or hidden by trees but you could always see the top of the house...or castle. It definitely had a gothic castle feel to it. Conor took my hands and led me up the stairs to the double doors. A man opened the door and stood to the side.

"Conor," he said with a smile. "I am glad you are not hurt."

"Thanks," he said to the butler. He had a fucking butler? We moved past him and into a large foyer.

"How fucking rich are you?" I found myself asking. Conor laughed before he led me up a flight of stairs. We must have walked past at least three doors before he opened a door into a very modern bedroom.

"Is this your childhood bedroom?" I asked him.

Conor smirked at me, that goddamn smirk I've been craving. "No. You'll never see that."

"Oh really?" I spoke. "Why? Do you have naked posters of Pamela Anderson in there?"

"No, she wasn't my childhood crush," he told me. "Was she yours?"

"Who wouldn't want her?" I told him, looking around. "So, whose room is this?"

"A spare one," he said quickly.

"Figures. I want to see it," I told him.

"Why?"

"Show me."

Conor shook his head, but that cocky little smirk was still present on his face. It was a welcome distraction from the bullshit I had just gone through.

"Let me see your wrists."

I looked down at them, realizing that they were bad. He crossed the room quickly and pulled my hands up so he could see.

"We need to clean these up," he told me. "Luckily, Walter was a medic in the army."

"Who is Walter?"

"The guy who opened the door for us," he told me. "He was a good friend with me da and he's looked after us our whole lives."

"Sure."

He went to the door and called down to Walter. My wrists still ached a little from the rubbing. The cold metal cuff wasn't helping.

Conor told me to come and sit down on the bed. He sat next to me and soon Walter came into the room.

"Can you check her wrists out?" Conor asked.

He nodded and came over to me, taking my fingers in his hands and lifting my hand up slowly.

"I'll need to clean these up," he said. "But first, I need

the cuffs cut off. Jye will be the best person to do that. He's arrived and is downstairs."

Conor nodded and Walter scuttled out of the room again. Moments later Jye came into the room with a tool in his hand.

"This isn't going to hurt, but if you move, it will burn you."

I nodded and held my wrists out for him. He took my hand in his while pushing a button on the tool and after a few moments, the tip was red. With a steady hand, Jye held the red tip over the cuff and I watched as it cut the metal to allow it to fall off my wrist. It landed on the ground with a clink. He went to work on the other one as Conor moved out of the room to take a call.

"Thank you," I told Jye as he released my second wrist.

"No problem," he smiled up at me.

"So you don't hate me like the rest of them, then?" I asked, looking down at my bloodiest and gross wrists.

"No," he said, pressing the button on the tool again. The red tip disappeared. "How can I hate someone I don't know?"

"You could hate me for taking Conor away from his work," I said. "Surely, he hasn't been the same since he met me."

"It's none of my business. He's my boss," he said. "The only time I'll hate you is if you break him."

"Sometimes men need to be broken," I told him. "Can't let you get your heads too full of fancy, now can we?"

Jye chuckled, something I could tell he didn't much of. "You may be right there."

He headed out of the room and Walter entered again. He had a bag in his hands that he put up on the bed next to me. When he opened it, I froze when I saw all the things in the medical bag.

"How bad is it?"

"Come to the sink," he said, leading me toward the bathroom. He held my hand under the spray, a sharp pain shot up my arm, but I bit down on my lip so that I didn't scream. The blood washed away to show that my wrist had a circular mark, the skin completely rubbed off the thin line of where the cuff was. "Now, the other."

I held my other hand under the sink and grit my teeth as the blood washed away to show a matching mark on the other wrist too.

"Not as bad as I first thought," he said. "Come, I'll put some bandages on them."

He led me back to the bed and put cream on the markings before wrapping them in gauze.

"Aspirin for the pain if required," he said before leaving. Conor came back into the room.

"You all good?" he asked me. "What did Walter say?"

"They aren't that bad," I said, holding my bandaged wrists up for him to see.

"Well good," he said. "My brothers called me. I was going to head down to the club to see what they want so you could get a nap in if you wanted."

"Sure, I could do that," I said, moving to the door. "But I wanted to see your room first."

"Not a chance."

"You know I could just start opening doors, I'm sure I can figure it out."

"Don't test me, woman."

I dodged his outstretched arm and ran out into the hall, opening the first door to reveal an identical room to the one we were in.

No, I was looking for a teenage boy's room. Conor was hot on my tail. I giggled as I ran to each door and opened it until I got to the last one. Conor had caught up to me and blocked my entry into the room.

"Oh, come on," I said. "What's the worst thing I'm going to find?"

"I think you need to have a nap."

I pushed him backward. He fell back into his room and I looked around. Heavy metal posters hung on the wall, and his quilt was black, actually everything was black in this room. Just like mine had been. What I expected was not this. I didn't expect him to be so much like me even at this age.

"Fine," he said finally. "You can have your nap in here but I can guarantee you, it won't be as comfortable as the other room."

I played at the edge of my shirt, and making a split second decision, I pulled my shirt off my body. His eyes grazed over my body, widening when he saw my lacy bra.

"Maybe you could help put me to sleep."

It didn't take much to get him to slam the door shut and close the distance between us. His hand was twisted into my hair, releasing the hair tie and flicking it to the side of the room. His fingers tangled in my curls as his mouth claimed mine. I felt every inch of his passion, every tiny bit of the relief of being back with him flooded me and I had to fight off the sobs that threatened. He unclipped the bra and let it fall between us to the floor, as he made a move to undo my jeans. His tongue was tangling with mine, sending my brain into overdrive. I could taste the whiskey on his tongue, not the cheap kind that I drank, but the rich stuff. The kind I couldn't possibly afford.

He pushed me up against the wall and broke apart from

me for a moment, breathing heavily as he yanked my jeans down and undid his own, pushing them down to the ground as well. He shoved his boxers down and moved toward me, his cock jutting out in front of him. He moved me over to his desk, turning me around so I could look out the window at the basketball court below as he moved his fingers into me from behind. I gasped as his cool fingers slid into me, my breathing laboring as he slowly, ever so slowly, massaged my pussy walls. I moved my legs wider, giving him the signal to fuck me senseless.

I wanted him to fuck me like he'd almost lost me.

Because, fuck, he almost had. I almost lost him.

It didn't take much more prompting on my part before he slid into me. Slow at first. I heard his sharp intake of breath as he tried to hold back.

But it didn't take long before he gripped my hips, digging those nails into my flesh and slamming into me, again and again.

I moaned as his cock stretched me from the inside. The feel of his velvety rigid cock gliding into me continuously had my body vibrating. He pushed one knee up over the desk for more room as he began to pick up the pace. His fingers tangled into my hair and pulled my head back. His mouth was on mine, our tongues tangling as he groaned into my mouth.

He pulled away as he increased his thrusting. I was on the edge, my pussy clenching around his cock. I screamed out as the orgasm hit me hard. He continued to pummel into me until my pussy began to release him. He pulled out of me much to my protest. He laid down on his bed and I climbed on top of him, looking down at his darkened eyes. The ones I dreamed about when I was held by Ronan. He held onto my hips as I began to ride him. My hair was bouncing round my shoulders, blocking my view of him on occasion.

I reached up and held my hair up with both my hands as he held onto my hips. I bounced on top of him, watching as his eyes widened and got even darker as he saw me biting my lower lip between my teeth.

He growled but he didn't try to push me underneath him. He let me do what I wanted and that thrilled me all over as I let my hair go and I put my hands over his pecs for leverage. I moved my hips into a circular rhythm, feeling his cock go all over inside of me, bashing into the sides of my pussy walls at all angles. I moaned as I felt him harden even more inside of me. I moved down to claim his lips in a simple kiss before I moved my butt up and down.

He growled right in my mouth as I did the move I'd never tried before. His hands were digging into my hips. The pain was piercing as I was sure his short nails had dug a hole into my skin.

I didn't care though. I needed him and all of him. I wanted him to mark me so that none other would ever consider me.

I was most definitely Conor's and he was mine.

As his breathing started to get short, I sat up and rode him harder and faster. Looking into his eyes as he came, something silent passed between us.

A silent agreement that this was it.

He was *mine*.

CHAPTER TWELVE

TEEGHAN

When I woke up, it was dark outside. I got dressed in some old clothes from Conor's wardrobe. A Metallica band shirt and some sweats, tying them tight around my waist, before I headed out to look for him. He'd left as I was falling asleep and promised to be back soon but I expected him to be back well before it got dark.

As I headed down the hall, I saw a familiar face exiting a bedroom.

"Sloane?"

She turned around, relief flooding her features as she ran at me. The last time I'd seen her, she'd been facing off with a masked man. I hugged her just as hard as she hugged me.

"Oh my god," she said in my ear. "I can't believe it. You're actually okay."

"Yeah," I said, realizing I should have called her the second Conor had brought me back here. I was a terrible friend. "It was Ronan."

"Ronan?" she repeated as she pulled back. "No way."

"Yeah, he and Conor really hate each other. He's one of the main players of the rebellion."

She shook her head. "That's just...fuck...who can you trust if not old friends?"

I shrugged, before realizing one major thing. She was in the O'Farrell's house. The same O'Farrell's she hated.

"Uh, Sloane, what are you doing here?"

"Oh," she said, a blush starting to head toward her cheeks as she tried to look at something to avoid looking at me. "Well after they took you, they suggested I stay here to be protected."

It made sense but it didn't make sense that she would take them up on it. She *hated* them.

"And you're still here?"

"Let's get something to eat," she said, turning to avoid eye contact again. I followed her down the stairs and down a corridor until we came out to a balcony. It was set up for dinner. Lorcan was sitting at the the end, reading something on his tablet. He didn't look up as Walter handed us a plate.

"The food is set up buffet style to the side," he said with a smile. "Help yourself."

"Uh, Walter," I said, softly. "Where's Conor?"

"He's still out, miss," he said. "Don't worry, he's with Jye and Killian."

I nodded and gave him a smile back before I headed over to the buffet table. The food looked amazing. Roast lamb, potato bake, vegetables, and bread. I piled my plate up and sat down with my back to the view. Sloane looked at the pile of food on my plate and shook her head.

"What?"

Lorcan looked up and then at my plate before he raised his eyebrows.

"Did I take too much?"

"No," Walter said, issuing a look to Lorcan who retreated back to his tablet. "You are more than welcome to fill up on as much food as you want."

"She's always been a big eater," Sloane giggled. "And yet she never gains weight. It's the most annoying thing in the world."

I caught sight of a slight smile from Lorcan before it disappeared. Blink and you'd miss it. Walter headed back inside and I tucked into the food, wondering how much longer Conor would be.

"Excuse me, ladies," Lorcan said as he headed inside with his empty plate.

"He seems like a grouch," I said to Sloane when he was gone.

Sloane shook her head. "Not really, but he does keep his feelings inside. Lorcan hasn't had the best life so far and he's always having to take control of shit Killian and Conor do. It's a full-time job."

"He doesn't have a woman?"

"No, he's not quite recovered from the girlfriend he lost years ago."

"What exactly does he do in the business?" I asked. "I know they split the responsibilities up when Finneas died."

"Yeah," she said, looking down at her food. "Well, Lorcan took the job that was the hardest to monitor. The brothels and porn business."

"Wow," I felt a chuckle rise. "No wonder he doesn't have a woman."

Sloane rolled her eyes. "Lorcan is a good man. He's the responsible one. Imagine having to be the big brother to both Killian *and* Conor."

"Good point."

I continued eating, listening to the sounds from the night air. It was so relaxing being here. I felt safe.

"I'm leaving tomorrow," Sloane announced suddenly.

"What?"

"I'm heading to the cottage Sean, and I bought," she said. "I'm going to do it up and sell it. I think I need to close the chapter on that."

I nodded. "I think you're well overdue but I get it."

"So you can come with me," she added. "But I know you won't."

I shook my head. "I need to be here."

"You're giving up on your hatred of Ireland so readily," she smiled. "I knew it would take one man to do that."

"It was never about hating Ireland. I love Ireland. I just didn't want to get stuck."

"And yet here you are, in the same town you feared so much."

"I feel like it's different now," I said, honestly. "My future feels clearer than being stuck in a dead end job like my mother and father had."

"Speaking of your father," Sloane said. "I didn't tell him you were taken because they swore until they were blue in the face they'd get you back safely but I think you should go and see him. Tell him about you and Conor."

She had a point. He did have a right to know although I heavily suspected he knew already.

"I'll tell him in a few days," I said. "I need to sort my shit out with Conor and figure out what we're doing and all that fun stuff."

Sloane smirked at me. "I think you already know there's no way you're getting out of being Conor's woman."

"I don't want to be out of it," I replied with ease. "We just need to figure out what we're going to do. Am I going to live with him or are we living here? What will I do to keep myself out of trouble, you know, those boring questions."

"Honestly, you don't have to worry about work," she told me. "Conor is loaded and he probably wouldn't mind having you stay at home, chill by a pool somewhere with a cocktail while he goes out and bloodies up some men."

I wasn't going to lie to myself, that sounded pretty fucking hot but I knew I'd get bored. I needed to be able to do something.

That was when I remembered.

"Did you know he brought Emma here?" I said, the anger still very much present in my tone.

"The Emma?" she asked.

I nodded.

"Why?"

"I guess because he killed Andrew, and he didn't want her to take the blame for it."

"That's actually pretty nice of him," Sloane said. "Conor doesn't usually have that much of a heart. Have you spoken to her?"

"No."

"Maybe you should, maybe he did to her what he did to you."

"She was my friend," I told her. "My best friend and she chose my husband over me. It's the ultimate crime to a friendship."

"I'm not saying it was right," Sloane said. "I just think you need to give her the benefit of the doubt."

I hated it when Sloane was right, which was always. She'd always had my back, and she'd always been the voice of reason.

But I still hated what Emma did to me. Emma had broken me.

· · ·

CONOR

I GOT BACK to the estate late, all the lights were off. The boys had kept me in a strategy meeting all fucking night. Lorcan had been his absolute worst tonight, annoyed that I hadn't caught on to the rebellion before now.

The fucker had his own business to run and yet he blamed *me* for not seeing it. He was a bigger asshole than our father was and that was saying something. I held my phone out and hit the torch on it before running up the stairs and to my childhood bedroom where she had insisted on staying.

That woman was going to be a permanent vex in my life...and honestly, I couldn't have imagined a better one to have.

I'd never fucked a woman in that room before, so for it to be her that I did it with, I was even happier. Slowly, I opened the door and looked over at her sitting up in my bed, reading a book.

"What are you reading?" I asked, putting my phone down and taking my shoes off.

"A book about snakes," she replied, showing me the cover. I remembered the book well. I'd begged my mother for it one Christmas, thinking I would escape the family business and run off to Australia to catch snakes. "Even though we don't have snakes in Ireland."

"I was obsessed with them," I admitted to her, taking off my jeans, and watching her gaze travel down to my cock. "Wanted to leave Ireland so I could go and catch them in Australia."

"Why didn't you?"

She tried to hide it, but I heard the deepness of her voice. She was turned on, yet again.

"I think you know the answer to that," I told her, before I pulled my shirt off. Her eyes were again appraising me like I was a prized bull. She put the book down on my bedside table and pulled her blankets down to reveal those glorious breasts. I climbed over her and got on the other side of the bed, against the wall.

"How did your big and important meeting go—ah, you probably can't tell me, hey?"

"I probably shouldn't," I told her. "But fuck it, it was a strategy meeting to deal with the rebellion. They've turned too many against us so we need to figure out what to do to assert our dominance again."

"What if I told you some things I overheard while I was being held?"

I looked at her, suddenly my mind was going crazy. I didn't want to push her to tell me about her time locked up, after all, her wrists were still heavily bandaged.

"You heard things?"

"Yeah, I heard them talking about people. I knew some names but not all of them. One name I remember vividly was Barry Murphy."

"Father Murphy?" I replied. "Are you sure?"

I fucking knew it.

"He was there. He never saw that I was there, but he knew I was, I could hear him telling them to get rid of me... that it would rattle you and bring down the empire."

I sat up, my mind buzzing. It made sense though, he was a pillar in the community, everyone followed him, everyone listened to him.

"That motherfucker."

I'd kept that fucker's secrets, our entire family trusted

him, our father trusted him and this whole time he'd been the one behind the rebellion. The O'Brien's were the face of it and he pulled their little fucking strings like a marionette.

I reached over her and grabbed my phone and dialed Jye.

"Get to the estate."

I hung up before Jye could respond and I reached over and kissed Teeghan hard. She moaned under the pressure of my lips on hers.

"We've been missing that link," I told her. "Thank you."

I jumped up and started to get dressed.

"What are you doing?" she asked. "It's two in the morning. Couldn't this wait?"

"No," I told her. "Sorry, I'll be back soon."

I reached down and planted another kiss on her lips before pulling my shirt on.

"Well then I'm coming down too."

"Hell no," I told her. "They ain't getting close enough to grab you again. They're going to pay for what they did to you, babe. I promise."

It didn't take long for Jye to get here. My brothers were both sitting down at the dining table already. Killian looked half dead but he knew this was important. Lorcan, I didn't think he slept anymore. No matter what time it was, he was always alert.

I told them what Teeghan had told me and what my suspicions had been.

"Could she be wrong?" Killian asked.

I understood why he was unwilling to believe it. I didn't want too either. Murphy had been the one who would counsel me when my father would beat the crap out of me for talking back, he would give me advice when I was being bullied by my brothers.

"I'm not wrong," I heard her voice from the top of the stairs. We all turned around and looked at her. She was slowly making her way down the stairs. "You think I wasn't horrified when I heard him referring to me and telling them to dump my body in the bay for Conor to find?"

Killian's face changed. I felt a fury build in me hearing it in those words. He had wanted to hurt me by killing her and letting me find her?

Murphy needed to go down.

"Jye, take Jimmy and Declan and watch him," I said. "I need to know who he sees, who comes in for confession, and every fucking move he makes."

Jye nodded and headed out the door without a backward glance. Lorcan had his arms crossed defensively, but I could see it wasn't because he didn't believe Teeghan, it was because he was hurt. He and Murphy had spent a lot of time together when father was still alive. Murphy and my dad had been close. It made me wonder how he could do this to his friends' sons.

"Come on," I said to Teeghan.

"I hate to say it, Con," Killian said. "But she knows things. We could get some more information out of her. She could be useful."

"No."

"Actually," Teeghan said. "I wouldn't mind getting it off my chest. If I can help you get rid of the rebellion, I would gladly do it. They fucked with my dad too. I hate them as much as you do."

"Unlikely," Lorcan said before moving away from us and heading into the dining room. I ushered Teeghan into the room and she took a seat. I sat next to her and Killian sat opposite us.

"Who else was involved in your capture?" Lorcan asked her.

All eyes were on her.

TEEGHAN

I'D NEVER BEEN to the docks before. Never had to but being here felt so strange. You instantly felt like you were in amidst something illegal.

I looked out at the placid bay. It was a nice day today, the storms had passed, and the skies were blue. It looked almost pleasant, save for the fact I could see the cottage where Ronan had kept me. Conor had told me Ronan had gotten away, that he hadn't been there when they'd burst in but they had killed a lot of his men. Except for Jakob.

That had been me.

And I didn't regret it once.

I could still recall the feelings I had felt when I shot him. Oddly enough I wasn't having nightmares about it nor did I feel bad. That wasn't normal, was it?

Then again he had been a fuckhead so he was asking for it, and the way he had hit me with the butt of his gun to knock me out pissed me off.

"You all, right?" I heard Jye ask me. He came to stand next to me, looking out at the bay.

"Just thinking."

"I come out here too to do it. The bay has a way of helping me come up with solutions."

"You always seem so put together, Jye."

He smiled. "Not always, but I never understood why

anyone would give away when they are rattled. In our business, it can mean life and death. You need to have a tough exterior and interior."

"I get that. I think I'm okay with that."

He chuckled. "You know he calls you Merida."

"Yeah, he told me," I laughed. "I don't mind Merida, she was a cool Disney character but I do have to remind Conor that she also chose not to choose a man."

"Only because she didn't need one," Jye said.

"No woman needs a man, she wants a man," I told him. "Most men think we need them."

Jye laughed. "You sound like me mam."

"Sounds like a wise woman."

"She is," he said.

"I'm surprised you know so much about Merida and Disney."

"It's a side effect of having a young daughter," Jye told me. I turned to look at him, surprised.

"You have a kid?"

He nodded. "Don't I look like a dad?"

"No, I mean, I guess I never thought about it but no," I replied, feeling bad.

"It's okay," he laughed. "I don't really want anyone to know that I have a daughter."

"I can understand that," I told him.

"So now you know I can trust you with something like that," Jye said. "If you hurt Conor, I will come after you because you know too much. Once you're in, you're in for life."

I smiled, because the fierce loyalty warmed my heart. Turning to him, I thought about how to respond before I finally realized what this was.

A test.

"If anyone hurt Conor, I would dismember them and use them to feed the fish in this very bay. If anyone pulled a Jakob on him though, and betrayed him from within the business, I would kill every member of their family, preferably in front of them before I let them stew on that guilt for months before I finally took their life."

I was startled by how dark that had gotten but I didn't want to show him that. I actually felt that I would get dark if someone tried to hurt Conor.

Jye smiled. "Good, I think you'll make it after all."

Conor joined us, putting his arm around my waist. "You want to go?"

"Actually," I said. "Can I see Jeremiah?"

Conor and Jye both shared a look, but for the life of me, I couldn't figure out what they were thinking.

"Why?" Conor asked me finally.

"I grew up with him and with Ronan. I want to confront him about what Ronan did to me."

Jye shrugged his shoulders. "I don't see why not."

I looked up at Conor and saw that he was contemplating it but finally he nodded. Jye led us down a row of containers stacked on top of each other until we got to a singular one. Jye opened it up, and I saw Jeremiah on a chair, chained to it, bloodied and bruised, the bright light that had suddenly invaded the room caused him to wince.

When he saw me, he got scared.

I liked how that felt. Stepping inside the container, I stood in front of him, Conor and Jye off to the side, and looked down at the man I had once called friend.

CONOR

I didn't know how I felt about this. Just a day after we rescued her, she wanted to face off with Jeremiah. As she stood in front of Jeremiah, silent, I could sense just how strong she was. She wasn't whimpering, nor had she cried since we got her back, instead she'd been resolute in wanting to hurt the rebellion. Lorcan didn't want to believe we could trust her, and had insisted we be careful with what we tell her. He always looked for the bad in people, just like father had.

"Jeremiah, look at me," she said, her voice hard as stone. He lifted his head slowly. "Did you know what he was going to do?"

"No," he croaked.

"We grew up together, Jer, you and I were like cousins," she said, still with no emotion in her voice.

Jeremiah was crying, I could see the clear lines through the caked blood on his face.

"Now, it's time for you to pay for your brother's sins," she said to him. She took a few steps back and picked up the bat we kept by the door. Without missing a beat, I watched as Teeghan swung the bat and landed it right in the middle of Jeremiah's chest. I tried not to look impressed but I knew my face would betray me. She beat the hell out of Jeremiah, while Jye and I watched on. I'd never been so turned on before, but I was thinking that a lot about Teeghan, every time she did something, I needed to be inside of her.

The chair fell over, and Jeremiah hit the floor with a thud. Teeghan finally stopped raining blows down on him, and stood back up. He was sobbing, sucking in deep breaths as Teeghan put the bat back down and looked over at us. I led her out of the dungeon, noticing she had specks of blood from the hits on Jeremiah all over her face. I wiped them off with my thumb.

"I'm really, really hot right now," I told her.

"Me too," she said.

"And that wasn't too much for you?" I asked her. She smirked up at me, and instantly I knew there was no way I could doubt it.

She was mine.

"No, Conor, I'm starting to realize just how angry I am."

"Good," I told her. "Use it."

"I have an idea," she said. Jye was closing the dungeon as he came over to us.

"What is it?"

"We know Murphy is a big player in this rebellion, right? What if I go to confession and tell him I'm scared of you and I need his help. I can say I have information he could use against you."

"That's too dangerous," I told her.

"She may have a point," Jye said. "There's no one else we could use, and it may be exactly what we need to use to trick him."

"No," I said, pacing. "You know how sick this motherfucker is. What if he figures out she is slipping us information?"

"We'll move in. I mean, she has proven that she can handle herself."

"He doesn't know I could hear him at the cottage," she said. "I have gone to confession so many times that it wouldn't be out of the norm. I'm going to do this, Conor. Whether you say yes or not."

Jye backed away from us, and headed back to the office. I couldn't believe she wanted to do this so soon after we rescued her.

"We'll find another way."

"I have an edge in, otherwise it will take you months to

get someone in. They know me, they know my father has had history with you guys. He will listen."

I couldn't breathe, this idea was so crazy. I didn't want to lose her again.

"I'll be fine, trust me."

There would be no way I could stop her. She was stubborn as fuck, just like I was.

"Fine, but the first sign of shit going down, you tell us and we'll come and get you."

She reached up and planted a kiss on my lips. I deepened the kiss and pulled her in close.

"But before you do go, we're fucking and hard."

She giggled as I pulled her up into my arms and carried her to the car.

CHAPTER THIRTEEN

TEEGHAN

I stepped inside the large church, the doors behind me creaking as they closed slowly. It must have been my nerves because I'd never heard them do that before. The sound was almost deafening. Conor and Jye would have lost sight of me and Conor was probably nervous as fuck but I couldn't focus on him right now. I had to focus on the plan.

My plan.

Father Murphy stood at the altar, looking over the candles that flickered in the darkened church. He slowly turned around when I continued to walk down the aisle toward him. I felt the fake tears run down my cheek. Much thanks to my dramatic teaching from high school, I could call on tears at any point.

"Teeghan?"

He was nervous, waiting for Conor to come out from the darkness behind me. He didn't know if he could trust this visit, and I could see it in his eyes. He still had a lot of fear over the brothers, just like everyone did. I wondered why he would have joined the rebellion if he feared them so much.

"Father, I must confess," I said, my voice wavering.

"My child," he held his hand out to usher me toward the confessional. "Come."

I stepped up to the confessional and entered through the other side to him. Taking a deep breath, I let it out slowly so the blood would stop pumping so hard in my ears.

I made the sign of the cross and said, "Bless me, Father, for I have sinned."

"Go on," he said, tentatively.

"I have slept with the devil," I lied. "I lusted over him and gave in to temptation but now I am scared, Father. He will not leave me alone and I fear I was recently taken by Ronan because of him."

He was silent for a moment, and I feared he may be on to me.

"You are not at fault, my child. The Lord will grant you forgiveness if you self-impose a ban on seeing him again. Do you feel you can do this?"

"I don't know, Father, he will not leave me alone. He kept me prisoner right after he rescued me, or so he says. I was better treated by Ronan."

Again, silence.

"I have a solution," he said, his voice a little less calming like it had been minutes before. My heart was racing. "But it will involve not speaking to anyone for a few weeks, not even to Sloane."

The mere mention of Sloane's name had the hairs on the back of my neck rising. He knew how to hurt me if he didn't believe me. My father and Sloane were the closest people to me. I had a lot to lose here. Sloane had already left for the cottage but it was no secret where it was. Sean had taken great pride in that cottage when they bought it.

"Please, Father, I will do anything."

"You have confessed, now I must have your rite of penance cited before I can give you solace."

I recalled the rite of penance we had been taught at school. "My God, I am sorry for my sins with all my heart. In choosing to do wrong and failing to do good, I have sinned against you whom I should love above all things. I firmly intend, with your help, to sin no more, and to avoid whatever leads me to sin. In his name, my God, have mercy."

"May our Lord and God, Jesus Christ, by the grace and compassion of His love for mankind, forgive you, my child, Teeghan, all your transgressions. And, I, His unworthy Priest, through the power given me, forgive and absolve you from all your sins, in the Name of the Father, and of the Son, and of the Holy Spirit."

"Amen," I finished, making the sign of the cross yet again.

He exited the confessional and I did the same. He took my hands in his, and I fought to pull away. His eyes were boring into mine to see if he could catch me in a lie but I was too strong for that. My vengeance would be swift but I had to wait for the most opportune time.

"Come, my child."

He led me through the private door behind the church and down a set of stairs that went underneath the church.

"You'll be safe here, but I do need your phone," he said, holding his hand out. "I cannot have you giving in to temptation, after all."

I handed him my phone. "Not even the O'Farrell's would dare to breach upon the church."

"Lord have mercy if they do," he said, a sinister smile on his face. I felt instantly on guard, but I didn't want to give in too early. I lifted my ankle up and brushed it against my other ankle, where the second phone was. The one Conor had insisted I take and hide in case he did take my phone.

I was still able to get word out from behind enemy lines.

Murphy locked the door to the church and rejoined me at the base of the stairs, his hand on my shoulder. I could feel how hard he was grabbing me as he led me down a darkened hallway.

I was so far underground, I realized, a little too late, that I may not get any reception.

CONOR

The door to the office was thrown open and a very angry Sloane came into the room, her rage evident. I stood up instantly. I knew she had already gone to the cottage. She'd told us she would be going so having her back here was a little unnerving.

"Where the hell is Teeghan?"

I didn't respond, wanting to know just what Teeghan had told her first.

"Can I help you?" Jye asked, almost sarcastically.

She shot him a look that I could only imagine made his cock shrink back into itself before she turned back to me.

"She hasn't answered her phone and now it's off," she said. "Tell me where she is."

"She's fine, Sloane," I said. "She'll call you when she's done."

"Done what?" she asked.

As if an angel had seen the plight I was in, my brother Killian walked in the door behind her. He was surprised to see her, and when he looked at me, he knew exactly what he had to do.

"Sloane," he said. Her anger dimmed a little when she heard his voice. Slowly, she turned around to face him. "Come with me."

She shot me another look of pure hatred before she finally left out the door. I walked out to the balcony to see Killian take her away so we couldn't hear what they were saying. Her arms were flying around every which way, she was furious, but Killian was speaking evenly without losing his cool. I wondered what had happened between the two of them all those years ago. I knew he had loved her, more than he had understood how to deal with, but all of a sudden, she was gone from our lives and we were forced to let her be.

No one disappears from our lives, once you loved one of us, that was it. Which was why I was hesitant to fall in love, but I didn't realize it could feel this good or this all-consuming. Sloane stormed off to her car and peeled out of the parking lot as Killian made his way to us.

His face was grim.

Something was wrong.

"We have a problem," he said as he approached us. "Get your asses in the car."

I grabbed Jye and we followed Killian from the docks to the main stretch of shops that faced the bay, specifically the Kennedy store. The shop had been blasted from the inside. Glass lay all over the ground, the shop completely burnt out. Police surrounded the area as we pulled up and that's when I saw it.

The body bag being wheeled out from the shop.

We continued down the street before the cops noticed us and parked at the picnic area near the water's edge. I got out and joined Killian on the bench overlooking the water.

"What the fuck happened?"

"Sloane told me the shop was bombed last night. Peter's dead."

I felt something akin to grief. Teeghan was going to be heartbroken. I knew for sure this had everything to do with the war between us and the rebellion.

"Who did it?"

"No one has taken responsibility," he said. "I called my contact at the police when I was in the car over here. They assumed it was us."

"Us?"

"The rebellion apparently have contacts too," he said. "We need to get this sorted, Con. It's fast becoming a bigger problem than I anticipated."

"Teeghan is working on it," I told him. "She said he's starting to ask her questions more, and tell her things about how the church is run."

"How much longer?" Killian asked. "We can't keep this from her forever. If they tell her, we may lose her as an ally."

I hated to think of her grieving for her father with that monster and not with me.

"I need to get her out."

"We'll lose our advantage," Jye cut in. "She wanted to do this because she knew she was the only one that could do it. Give her the benefit of the doubt. She has darkness in her, we've seen it, Conor."

"She does?" Killian enquired.

"More than I could have imagined," I told him.

"Well, that's a good thing," Killian said. "Well, I guess time will tell just how much darkness she has in her."

He got up and headed back to his car. Jye took his seat

on the bench and we sat in silence as I tried to mull over a million ways we could get her out and still have an advantage, but I knew Jye was right. She had chosen to do this and I had to trust she had it in her.

"I don't want her finding out about her dad," I said.

"Then let's hope we can scare the rebellion a little, help sell the story that she is scared of us."

I felt the smile creep up on my face. A little hell raising couldn't hurt and it would take my mind off whatever the hell my brain was trying to process.

"Let's go," I said, as we headed to the car.

TEEGHAN

Ronan's eyes widened when he saw me walking into the room with Father Murphy. I had to fight not to launch at him for all the shit he put me through just a few days ago.

"Are you fucking kidding me?" he shot at me. "You can't trust her, Murph."

"Be quiet," Murphy spat back. "You are the one who rushed our plans, and screwed them. Now, we have someone who has been feeding us information on the O'Farrell's."

"They still have my brother, maybe she should tell me how to get him back," Ronan said, giving me the most evil glare imaginable.

"Ronan, we used to be friends," I said, as innocently as I could muster. "And you are the one who locked me up. I don't know why you would be so cruel given how close we used to be."

He didn't respond, but I could tell he didn't believe me. He sat down at the table, and Murphy showed me through to the kitchen to make a coffee. Murphy and Ronan spoke in hushed tones, and I knew they were arguing over me. I quickly got to work making a coffee, trying to listen for any keywords I could use against them.

"Taking a long time in there," Ronan called out. I dropped the spoon in the sink with a clunk and headed back out.

"Sorry, I like a good stir," I told him. "Father, I'll be in the quarters you showed me."

Murphy waved me off and I headed down the hall, looking closely to see how many people were around the compound. Murphy had shown me a tunnel from the church to this little cottage out the back of it which is where he lived. I didn't even know this place existed, no wonder it was where the rebellion came to discuss things. I put the coffee down on the small table by the door of the small room he had me in, and I entered another door in the cottage. It was a library of sorts, lots of old books and record books, probably the town records. I quickly ducked inside and looked through the record book that was open. Sitting down, I looked at the family tree that I could see was the O'Brien's. It was strange because Paul O'Brien was the last entry. Ronan and Jeremiah weren't listed.

I flicked it over and saw the O'Farrell's with the subtitle 'Founder' of our little community next to the top name, Cathal. The O'Farrell's had ruled our community since the beginning, probably with as much force as they did now, but if they didn't, we probably wouldn't have made it through the IRA attacks. They chased them out a long time ago. My heart did a little flutter when I saw Conor's name at the bottom. Flipping the pages back, I saw the Kennedy's and looked down at my name, but there was something off about it. The names under my mother weren't just Sean and myself, Ronan and Jeremiah also appeared under her name but not my father's name.

What the actual fuck?

I heard footsteps heading my way so I escaped out of the room and into my quarters, my heart racing and my mind fuzzy. How could Ronan and Jeremiah be on my family tree? They were O'Brien's.

I sipped my coffee and sat on my bed, my heart racing with what I'd just seen. Father Murphy appeared at my open door, and I faked a smile so he didn't suspect anything.

"Come with me," he said, with a smile. "I've something to show you."

I put my coffee mug down and followed him, my stomach aflutter and my heart racing a mile a minute. Thank God he couldn't hear that, although by the rushing of blood in my ears, it was loud.

He led me out of the cottage and down a narrow pathway to what looked like a mausoleum. I hadn't texted Conor yet today, I had been hoping to hear something worthy of telling him but by doing that he may think something had gone wrong and bust in.

All of this would have been for nothing.

Hopefully he had faith in me to do what I needed to do.

He unlocked the doors to the ancient looking mausoleum and we stepped inside. It wasn't dusty and gross like I expected, rather it was clean and well looked after.

"What is this place?" I asked him, looking around for any identifiable marker of who this place housed. That's when I saw the name O'Farrell engraved on a plaque that hadn't been cleaned in some time. It was the only thing in this room that was unclean. Murphy moved a tapestry of the four leaf clover and opened a door. The hair on the back of my neck rose and I felt bad about this but I couldn't chicken out now. They were expecting me to give them intel. I had to keep doing that.

I followed him in through the door, even though my legs did not want to carry me. The next room we entered was cold, and dark. One single light was dim and hanging from the ceiling. The room had three doors all around the circular room.

"You know Conor has been holding on to a secret of mine," he said, his voice taking on a different tone. A tone that had chills shooting up and down my spine. My flight response was being triggered but I stayed put. "And he's kept something of mine that he had no right to."

"What is that?"

He smiled, a vicious little smile that really should have told me to run but he turned to unlock the door. As the door creaked open, I saw the secret Conor held over him. Two girls sat huddled in the corner of the room, a cuff on their ankles, chained to the center of the room. They looked frightened.

Murphy brushed his hand against my hair and tucked it behind my ear. He leaned closer, and I fought everything in me not to run. "You'll make a nice payment for what the boys took from me."

I turned to see his hand coming up against my head and suddenly I felt myself falling.

CHAPTER FOURTEEN

CONOR

"Something's wrong," I said to Jye as I looked at my phone. "She hasn't messaged me this morning."

"She may not have the chance to," he offered, but I could see he didn't believe what he was saying. "Give her a couple more hours."

I put my phone down but I could feel something was off. My chest burned with anxiety.

Lorcan entered the office. He never came down to the docks, so this wasn't going to be good. Killian was behind him, and he had a telling look on his face.

"Release Jeremiah to Ronan," Lorcan said.

"Why? That's the only leverage we have on them."

"I don't want anything else to happen in this town. We need to call off this goddamn war. Ronan will stop if his brother is returned to him."

"Are you really that stupid?" I asked him, getting up from my desk.

"We have to try," Killian said. "They bombed one of our

clubs."

That had been news to me. "Which club?"

"Does it matter?" Lorcan bit back. "Release him."

"No," I told him. "I don't tell you how to run your side, you don't tell me how to run my side. I have things I could lose too, you know. You need to learn to respect me and the business I run."

We stood, face to face, not one of us stepping back. Killian moved to separate us, knowing just what could happen if you crossed me. His own face was still healing from the beatdown I gave him.

"Come on," Killian said, shoving us apart. "This isn't helping."

"I am not fucking giving Jeremiah up."

"He in a good condition?" Killian asked me.

I shot him a look which was all he needed to know that Jeremiah was not going to be in good condition if we handed him over.

"Do you have any fucking leads?" Lorcan asked me.

Killian shot me a look to tell me that it wasn't best to tell him I had been raising hell with the rebellion members. He would be pissed off and that would last weeks.

We didn't have weeks, we needed numbers to defeat these motherfuckers.

"How is Teeghan going?" Killian changed the subject. "What intel has she given today?"

"Nothing as yet."

Killian frowned. "Doesn't that concern you? She's been giving you information every morning."

"A little, but I need to trust in her plan. She's tough as they come."

"If she melted your ice-crusted heart, I've no doubt."

My phone dinged and I looked over at it. Jye read the message.

"She has no news today but she's going to spy on a meeting tonight."

"So, there won't be any rebellion members out tonight if they are holding a meeting," Lorcan said. "We should try and break into Ronan's house."

I nodded. "Sounds good. I wouldn't mind fucking it up."

"You aren't coming," Lorcan said. "You're obviously a liability. We don't want to let him know we've been there. Stay here and deal with your containers."

He said it with a sneer. He'd always hated the docks, even when father had forced him to learn the business in case he died early. Luckily, he'd died when we were old enough to take over.

Killian and Lorcan left my office, and I was angry. I picked up the closest thing to me and threw it at the wall, leaving a large hole.

Jye handed the phone to me and I looked down at the message. "She used emojis."

"And?"

"Teeghan doesn't use emojis. She's never used them when we texted."

I quickly scanned the rest of our texts to make sure I wasn't going crazy but he was right, not one emoji. She also spelled everything out, there were no shortened words. This message had u rather than you, and 2night instead of tonight.

"This isn't her."

My heart hammered in my chest. I fucking knew I shouldn't have let her go. That motherfucker, the sick motherfucker, had my girl.

"He doesn't know we know," Jye said, breaking me from

my murderous thoughts. "We could use that, give him false information back."

"I need her back here," I said. "We have to get her out."

"Surely he has her hidden somewhere."

"Then we need to find someone who will know where he would hide her."

Jye nodded and grabbed the keys to the dungeon. I felt the rage building. If that motherfucker touched Teeghan, I would grind his guts up and feed them to him.

TEEGHAN

MY HEAD WAS POUNDING as I opened my eyes. The dim light in the room I was in didn't hurt my eyes so that was a plus. I pulled myself up from where I lay on the floor, hearing the noticeable sound of chains pulling. I looked down at the cuff on my ankle and the chain connected from the side of it to the center of the room I was in.

Panic set in.

Murphy had locked me in the room with his sex slaves. I looked down at my clothes and noticed they weren't disturbed.

"He did not touch you," someone said. I looked up and saw the two girls from before in the corner. They looked dirty, like they hadn't bathed in weeks and they were frail.

"But he will," the other one said. Their accents were thick, if I were to take a guess I'd say Russian.

"Don't say that, Mira," the first one hushed the other.

"Are you from Russia?"

They both nodded.

"How long have you been here?" I asked them.

"We don't know."

"We don't see sunlight," the one named Mira said. She seemed to be the pessimist of the two of them. "This light above us has UV in it. He wishes to keep us healthy enough to have his way with us until we get pregnant."

"What happens then?" I asked her.

"I don't know," she said. "The last girl that was here was pregnant and he took her away once she started to show."

How could Father Murphy do this? He had been the man who ran Sunday School, and all our services. He had presided over my mother's funeral, and my brother's wedding. He was friends with my father.

God. What would my father be thinking? He hadn't heard from me in days. Hopefully he had assumed I had gone to London like the original plan had been.

"How did you end up here?" I asked them.

"We were bought," Mira told me. "Our families were poor, my father lost me in a gambling debt repayment. I was shipped here, offered a new life with a new husband."

"Alina was here when I arrived."

"My mother had found me an Irish husband so she was told," Alina said. "She told me to keep my mouth shut and be a good girl or I'd end up in an abusive marriage like hers."

"That sounds awful."

"When you got here, how did you get in here?"

"At first," Alina started. "He was so kind, he fed us, and because of who he was he thought maybe he would introduce us to our husbands in a few days after we got clean and all."

"But after two days of pleasantries," Mira said. "He told me he was going to show me something. I was excited, and nervous, but when he brought me into this building, I knew something was wrong. He hit me over the head when I tried to run and I woke up in here. Alina was here when I woke up."

"I am sorry you have gone through that. But we will get out of here. There are people I can contact to come in and help us."

I reached down for my phone tucked into my ankle, but it was gone.

"He took it," Alina offered. "He was not happy you had it."

Oh shit.

There was no way for me to tell Conor what had happened, or that we were locked up in here. I hoped like hell that after no response from me he would burst in and find me before Murphy had a chance to hurt these girls again.

"There were other rooms," I said. "What's in them?"

"Other girls," Alina said. "We can hear them crying sometimes."

"How many girls does he have?"

"We don't know, it changes, some girls leave, and some girls come," Mira said. "It is not just him, he lets his men have fun sometimes."

The shame on their faces was enough to make me murderous. I was going to kill that motherfucker when he showed his face again.

I knew one thing was for sure. He would not break me.

I would break him.

Mira and Alina were dozing in and out of sleep as I tried to find a way to get the cuff off me. The chains rattled constantly and they jolted a little in their sleep but they didn't wake up. I wondered how long they had been here.

I heard footsteps outside and I sat back against the wall, bracing for what was to come. The door opened and I saw Murphy standing there, with a sick smile on his face.

"I see you've woken," he said.

"Fuck off," I spat.

"Come now," he said. "That's no way to speak to your priest."

"You ain't a priest," I shot at him. "How could you do this to women?"

"Easily, it turns out," he shrugged his shoulders as if this was an everyday conversation. "I didn't expect I'd ever end up with a beauty such as yourself, Teeghan, but I'm happy to add you to my collection."

Collection.

He was a sick fuck.

"Come on," he said to me, coming into the room. The other girls looked at me with horror as he hauled me to my feet. "It's time for me to sample the goods."

My stomach lurched with what was left in it but I held onto it. I tried to fight him, but he hit me hard in the side of the face, leaving my vision blurring. I leant over, my stomach threatening to empty, as he undid my cuff and dragged me out of the room. Alina and Mira were protesting for him to leave me alone but all I could feel was the pain in the side of my head, as I looked up at the ceiling of the mausoleum as he dragged me into yet another room. The dizziness was fading as I looked around at my surroundings. This room had one bed on it, and realization hit me hard.

He was going to put his sick and perverted hands on me and rape me.

Hell no.

I looked everywhere for a weapon I could use. Murphy wasn't going to get me, no way in hell.

CONOR

Jye and Declan stood on the side of the church, as I loaded my gun and headed inside with Jimmy and Killian. We took in our surroundings quickly before we headed for the door that Murphy used all the time. Quickly, we made work of the door and headed down a hallway that I knew led to his quarters.

Only, we came to a tunnel that took us further underground before we came to an opening. Confused, I looked to Killian who shrugged his shoulders. We moved through the gate and into a garden. I could have confused it for the Garden of Eden but I knew it wasn't. Murphy was a sick fuck, I'd known it for over a week, although I'd had my suspicions earlier on. I never should have let Teeghan do this.

Jeremiah had given up information on where Murphy kept his girls. As we looked around the garden, I saw the mausoleum where he had told me was his sex dungeon. If Murphy fucking laid one hand on Teeghan, I would end his miserable existence. Jye and Declan took the mausoleum as I saw men coming out of a cottage. Jimmy, Killian and I ran at them, aiming our guns as they retreated back into the cottage. Motherfuckers were going to die in a hail of bullets.

I looked for Ronan everywhere but I couldn't find him. Killian had his silencer on his gun, and he shot at the three men in quick succession.

"Take all the fun out of it, why don't you?" I shot at him.

"Go and get your girl," Killian said. "We got this."

I nodded and headed over to the mausoleum.

TEEGHAN

I could hear him getting ready to rape me from behind. I didn't dare turn around. All I knew was this was not going to happen to me. I slowly slid off the bed he'd put me on and looked for something to use.

It's like he knew something like this could happen, that a woman would dare to defy him and there was no weapon in here. I turned around to see him standing there without his cassock on.

"Thank you God," I said. "I really didn't want to sully that cassock."

Murphy's face changed and I did what my brother had taught me in school when I had developed breasts seemingly overnight.

He was coming for me, anger in his eyes, and I used my shin and I kicked upward between his legs. Murphy stopped immediately, his eyes all but bulging out of the sockets as he fell to his knees.

I must have done some kind of permanent damage because even my shin hurt. I limped out of the room and toward the door he had taken me from. It was locked.

I tried with everything I had to get the door to open but it was no use. I started to hobble back to Murphy to get the keys, hoping like hell he was still unable to move, when I heard the door to the mausoleum burst open.

God, were his men here looking for him?

I was about to hide when I saw Jye's face appear, his gun drawn. The second he saw me, he lowered the gun.

"Teeghan? Are you all right?" he asked me.

"I am, but I need to get these girls out."

"Come on, I'll come back for them."

"No," I said, firmly. "They come with us now."

He nodded. "Okay, where's Murphy?"

"On his knees in the other room."

Jye smirked at me. "Did you even need us to rescue you?"

I shrugged. "Maybe, maybe not."

I was about to run back in there when Jye stopped me. "What are you doing?"

"Getting the key."

"Fuck that," he said. He moved to the door and shot at the lock. The door opened instantly.

"Still need the key for the chains, brainiac," I shot at him. He rolled his eyes and moved to the girls. I stood at the door.

"It's okay," I told them. "He's here to help us."

They relaxed a little as he shot at the chains connecting them to the floor and helped them up.

"Are you okay to walk?" he asked them. They both nodded and I helped them toward the door.

"The others," Alina said, pointing to another door.

"I got them," Jye's friend said as he headed to the door and shot at the lock.

"Get them out," Jye told me. "I'll bring Murphy's ass out."

I helped the girls through the door and out into the daylight. Alina and Mira both winced at the bright light that they hadn't seen in weeks. Killian was coming out of the cottage, his gun in his hand.

"What a sick fuck," he said to no one in particular.

"Killian, can you take them to the car?" I asked. He nodded and took their hands as they headed out through the tunnel and back into the church.

Conor came out of the cottage next, a gun in his hand, relaxed. When he saw me, his eyes changed from anger to relief. He crossed the distance between us quickly and took me in his arms, his mouth on mine.

"Did he hurt you?" he asked once we parted.

"No, he didn't get the chance. I nailed him in the balls."

He snorted and laughed. "That's my Merida."

I rolled my eyes at the nickname he'd given me as Jye hauled Murphy out onto the ground with a grunt. The other guy, whose name I didn't know yet, was leading four girls out that he'd rescued from the other room.

"Jesus."

"He wasn't here today," I told Conor. "I think he must have given up on Murphy a long time ago."

Murphy was still groaning about his balls which made me giggle.

"What you want to do with him, boss?" Jye asked.

The girls were being led past us, in tears, and out of sight.

"Thanks Dec," Jye said.

Conor handed his gun to me. "He's not mine to kill."

I felt the weight of the gun in my hand, and damn didn't it feel good. As I moved toward the lump of shit that I looked up to in my childhood, I could see the real fear in his eyes.

The same fear he probably laughed about when he saw it in those girls' eyes right before he raped the fuck out of them.

I aimed the gun between his legs and shot. The scream that came out of him had me smirking.

"Was that the left ball or the right one?"

Conor and Jye both looked at me as if I were crazy, and yet with a level of respect I never thought I would see.

"Ah hell," I said. "Why leave the other out?"

I shot again. He was howling in pain, blood spewing out of his underwear and onto the green grass below him.

"You bitch," he spat at me.

"Sounds like you're the one being a bitch right now, Murphy."

I shot at his chest, aiming for a lung. It forced him back onto the ground, writhing in pain. He was beginning to spit up blood, a slight gurgle becoming prevalent. I looked down at his hands, clutching at the grass below him. Those same hands that had raped innocent women.

I shot at his left hand. He howled again, blood dribbling down his chin.

"Finish him," Conor said.

"No," I replied, turning back around and handing him the gun. "He can drown in his own blood."

"Savage," I heard Jye say under his breath as we turned and headed toward the church.

CHAPTER FIFTEEN

CONOR

Tee got out of the shower, a towel wrapped around that body that I couldn't seem to get out of my mind when we weren't together. Her vibrant red, curly hair was wet and down over her shoulders.

"Feel better?" I asked her. She hadn't told me what had happened at Murphy's compound yet and I was honestly a little scared to find out the truth. Given how she reacted in the garden, I had to figure he'd hurt her bad.

"Lots," she replied with a smile. "Where are the girls?"

"The ones we rescued?" I enquired.

She nodded.

"They're at the estate, getting a hot shower and some food. I asked Emma to get them some clothes."

"Emma is here?" she asked me, dropping the towel and revealing that perfect body. I felt all the blood leave my brain and head south. My cock was hard instantly pressing against my jeans.

"Hello?" she waved a hand in front of my face as she pulled on her panties. "Earth to Conor."

"Sorry," I said, looking up into her eyes again. "You can't expect a man to think when you drop a towel like that."

She rolled her eyes and continued getting dressed.

"Wait...what did you mean the ones we rescued...what other girls would I be talking about?"

Shit. Conor and his big mouth again.

"Murphy had a container come in a week ago. We opened it when he was being shady, and we found two girls he had shipped here."

Her eyes widened. "What? Another two?"

"Yes."

"And you knew what a sicko he was?"

"I didn't know the depravity, no, and I surely didn't think he was involved with the rebellion. The girls were being looked after by Jye's mam but since we have more now, I thought we could house them here. We have enough rooms and plenty of food. Emma is simply helping."

"Why her?"

"She's got some trauma from Andrew as well. You should talk to her."

"What about the others?" she asked me. "Are they going to get homes? They're obviously not legally allowed to be here."

"Sure. We'll sort that out."

"They'll be damaged from their ordeal. I don't know how to help them."

"We do. Well, my brother told me about this thing my father did when he found women who had been abused. He would train them, teach them how to protect themselves, and maybe become part of his army. It gave them a purpose and a way to let out their rage."

"I thought your dad was an asshole."

I sighed. "He was but he also had a heart when it came to women, unless it was staying faithful."

Teeghan pulled her hair up in a bun and looked at me. "What now?"

"Teeghan, sit down," I told her, patting the bed beside me. "I have to tell you something."

She was hesitant but finally she sat down on the bed next to me. "What is it?"

"The day before we rescued you, we found out someone had bombed your father's shop."

Her breathing changed and she started to look off into space. "Was he in there?"

She already knew. I could see it in the way she was fighting off tears. "Yes."

"Who was it?"

"Ronan, I presume."

"Why my father?"

"I don't know, I guess because he wanted to make an impact. He knew I would do anything for you and if he hurt you, he would hurt me."

She fell to her knees, her chest rising and falling rapidly as she held back her cries of pain. The grief was hard to see on her.

"Cry, babe, let it out."

"I won't cry. That's what he wanted...unless he got rid of him to keep his secret."

"What secret?"

She wiped the tears from her cheeks and stood up, turning to face me. "When I was in the cottage, I found his record books or the town's record books really. They have family trees for every family there. Especially the earliest families, like the Kennedy's, O'Brien's and the O'Farrell's."

"Sure, I knew that."

"Well, I looked at the O'Brien's page and Ronan and Jeremiah are not on there under Paul. I figured it just hadn't been updated but when I looked at my family tree, they were listed under my mother's name."

"What?"

"It states they are my half-brothers, not my father's sons. Sean and I were under my parents like normal. I guess my father knew."

"Why would they need to hide that?" I asked her, my mind a maze of curiosity. "Why would Paul raise them as his own?"

"I don't know, but if he was their father, they would appear on his page, wouldn't they?" she asked.

"It can't be the reason they killed Peter," I said. Teeghan's eyes began to water again. I pulled her into my arms and held her tight. We laid down on the bed and I just held her, letting her silent sobs shake through her entire body. She had no family left now.

Only me.

I couldn't imagine what life would be like with no family left.

When Teeghan finally fell asleep, I crept off the bed, pulling the blanket up and over her before I walked out the door.

I texted Jye as I headed to my car and told him to meet me at the docks.

Jye turned up after a few minutes as I stood outside the dungeon. Once he got to me, I unlocked the container and let the light shine in on Jeremiah. He had been healing well since the last time we beat the hell out of him.

"Teeghan just told me your secret," I said to him, as Jye and I entered the dungeon. "Why is it such a secret?"

"What?" Jeremiah croaked, looking up at me from his spot on the ground. We'd undone his chains and given him food and water every day to keep him alive so he was able to form enough words to respond to us.

"Don't lie."

"I don't know what you're fucking talking about."

"Your brother killed Peter Kennedy," I said quickly. I watched his response and was surprised when he looked shocked.

"He wouldn't do that."

"He did."

"No, I don't believe you."

I sighed, knowing this was going to go over Jeremiah's head. "It couldn't be the fact Peter knew the secret about you and your brother?"

"What secret?" Jeremiah asked. "What are you talking about?"

He didn't know.

Ronan really did keep him in the dark about everything. He hadn't even tried to save him even though he knew exactly where he was.

"There's something I need to tell you, Jeremiah, but this isn't the place. Get up."

Slowly, Jeremiah stood up, his balance unsteady as he made his way over to us. Jye helped him out of the dungeon, his eyes immediately closing under the light from outside. Jye put him in the back seat of his car.

I got in the passenger seat and Jye got in beside Jeremiah. I was about to blow his world right apart.

TEEGHAN

This place was a maze. How the hell did anyone find where they were looking for? I turned yet another corner and came face to face with the one person I didn't want to see.

Lorcan.

His gruff appearance told me I was the last person he wanted to see as well.

"Sorry," I said. "I'm looking for the exit. I need to go and get some food."

"We have a kitchen here," he said. "It's down that hall and to the left."

"I was hoping for a pub meal," I told him. "It's been a fucking long and torturous week."

He relaxed a little bit. "I know what you mean. Is O'Laughlin's okay?"

"You're going to take me?" I asked, surprised.

He nodded. "I don't want you to get kidnapped again, so I'll come with. I could murder a pint myself."

The way he had said murder was direct and oddly enough scary, and yet it had been humorous too.

"Sure."

He led me out to the driveway where a range of cars were parked off to the side. They were all gorgeous cars, and probably cost a pretty penny too. He walked over to one of them and I got in beside him. It felt weird leaving the estate with Lorcan and not with Conor or Killian. I knew Lorcan didn't like me, so I could easily be walking into a trap but I had to have faith.

Someone did.

"Are you okay?" he asked me as we headed into town.

He didn't look at me, but I could tell he was asking about my dad.

"No, but I guess we all go sometime."

"That is true."

We got to O'Laughlin's and Lorcan parked outside, in a no parking zone. I couldn't help but smile at his devil may care attitude as he waited for me to walk inside. Everyone turned to look at me, obviously well aware that my father just died.

The owner, Phelan, looked at me with sadness, which turned to surprise and a little fear when they saw Lorcan come in behind me. Everyone's eyes turned away as Lorcan led me to a booth in the back.

"What do you want?" he asked.

"Pie and a beer."

He nodded and headed to the bar. Phelan served him quickly and he returned with my beer and his Guinness. I may have been Irish, but I couldn't stand the stuff. He was silent as we drank, but I couldn't get over how much he looked like Conor, just a little older. His hair was starting to grey at the sides.

"What?"

"I only just realized how much you look like Conor."

He rolled his eyes. "Well, I wouldn't have expected you to be looking at me so intently, so the surprise is normal I suppose."

Phelan brought out my pie and a burger for Lorcan. As I tucked into the pie, I thought of the life I would undoubtedly have now. My own family was gone.

Everyone, my brother, my father, my mother. Sloane was at the cottage so I wouldn't see her much until she was done down there. I knew it was to get away from Killian. I'd seen the way they looked at each other. It was almost like they were each other's forbidden fruit.

"Why didn't you all go to school together?" I finally asked. It had surprised me as well; I didn't even realize I'd been thinking about it.

"We couldn't get along," he said. "Always fighting, so when Conor was old enough for school, the school begged our mother to split us up."

I stifled a giggle. "She must have had hell with you three."

"That's putting it mildly."

"I remember Killian from school, but not you or Conor."

He nodded. "That's why. Why did you leave Ireland all those years ago?"

"A few reasons but the main one was that I met and married an Englishman."

Lorcan screwed his face up which caused me to laugh and almost spill my beer.

"I wish I'd known what a waste of time it would have been then."

"Did he hurt you?"

"Only emotionally," I said. "He cheated but I guess I never truly loved him, he was a means to an end."

As if on cue, I looked at the woman walking into the pub and my smile dropped. I looked away just as she made a move to look our way. Lorcan noticed it.

"She's the one, isn't she?" he asked.

I nodded. "She was my best friend."

"Ouch," he replied. "She's done good with the girls and she's always polite but I can see she is harboring some secrets that I don't think she's ready to face."

"What do you mean?"

Lorcan sighed. "You may not see it because you hate

what she did but she's a broken woman, Teeghan. Maybe you need to have it out so it doesn't eat you up inside. Find closure. I'm not saying be friends again, but you both need to speak to each other."

We sat in silence again as we finished our meals and I finished my beer.

"Another?" he asked.

"Sure."

He went to go and buy another round. While I waited for him to return, Emma came over to the table.

"Hi," she said weakly.

"Hello."

"I just want you to know that once the girls are healthy and settled, I'll find my own place. I don't want you to feel like you have an enemy around you."

I could feel the sadness in her. Maybe Lorcan was right. Maybe, just maybe, I could forgive her. After all, she got me away from the asshole husband I had married.

"Sit down."

I looked over at Lorcan who was talking to someone at the bar. He'd planned it once he saw her walk in.

I had to give it to him. That was crafty.

She did, tentatively.

"I know I went nuts on you back at the apartment," I said. "Conor told me what he did. He told me you weren't the bad one and that I should take it easy on you."

"He's a good man," she said. "I'm glad you found someone who treats you properly."

"I can see Andrew left his mark on you too," I said.

"You don't see the scars he left on me," she said. "He always made sure you couldn't notice it."

I remembered how sick Andrew could be when he was drunk. He knew he hadn't been able to push me too far after the first time. I'd kicked him so hard in the junk that he'd not been able to walk for two days. Emma had never been that way. She didn't have it in her sweet disposition to tell him where to go.

"You just took it?" I asked her.

She nodded. "I wanted to make him happy. He had somehow talked me into thinking I was the woman he'd been after all this time."

"He was a master manipulator," I told her. "You should have–"

I stopped when I was about to say *called me* but I knew I wouldn't have helped her. I had blamed her.

"I'm sorry," I told her, and I meant it.

I could see the water in her eyes, threatening to spill over. "Thank you."

"Stay as long as you want," I said quickly. "There's nothing worse than feeling like you need to go when you're not ready."

She smiled a little, but it was a battle heavy smile. "Thank you."

She slid out of the booth and went over to the bar to get a drink. As Lorcan was making his way back, I noticed that the entire pub had seemingly emptied.

When he slid back into the booth, I asked him, "Do you like the fact you can empty a pub just by being here?"

He looked around and shrugged. "It's not my fault they're scared of me."

"Maybe it is."

He rolled his eyes as he took a sip of his drink. "I had my doubts about you, but you've exceeded them all, I must say."

"Is that your mark of approval?" I asked, hoping like hell he wouldn't stand in the way of me and Conor.

"He doesn't need my approval to date you," he said.

"Even still, I'd like to know."

"It takes a lot out of your soul to do what we do," Lorcan said after a brief silence. "We never asked to be born to him, but we took on the family legacy because we had to. Women don't tend to understand that or so I've seen."

"What happened to you?" I asked him. "A girl did something to you."

He smirked, looking down at his pint. "It's always a girl, isn't it?"

"Well?"

"Jesus, you're pushy."

"You ain't seen nothing yet."

He smirked but tried to hide it quickly. "She left me."

"Because of what you do?"

He nodded. "She couldn't stomach it. I'd even thought I would leave the business for her but she told me she was getting married to another man."

"Ouch," I said.

"A few years later, I found out he had killed her so I tend to steer clear of relationships. They burn you pretty bad when it doesn't work out."

"Sometimes," I offered. "And sometimes, women can surprise you."

Lorcan nodded. "So, it appears with you and Conor. I never thought I'd see that boy settle down."

I shrugged my shoulders. "I do what I can."

He chuckled. I made Lorcan O'Farrell chuckle. It was such a genuine and manly chuckle too, one you didn't hear too much.

"I hope you and Emma were able to talk."

"Subtle," I replied. He smirked at me. "Yeah, it made me realize that I'd left her with the guy who I was desperate to get away from. I never loved Andrew. Sometimes I forget that and I get angry that I didn't have control over my life. Emma had it bad. She was never as feisty as me."

"Come on," he said. "I better get you back before Conor sends a party out to murder me."

I finished my beer and took his lead out to the car. That's when I saw it. My father's shop, completely blown to bits.

Lorcan realized what I was looking at and came to stand next to me.

"Don't worry, Teeghan. We're going to fucking get him."

I got in the car and we took off back to the estate, my mind a flutter. I knew the place had been blown up but I didn't quite realize the devastation of it until just now.

Ronan had blown my father up.

Ronan was going to fucking die in a fiery inferno.

CONOR

The car pulled up to the doorway just as Jye and I got out of our car. Lorcan got out and then Teeghan. Instantly my heart did something weird and then my anger took over.

"Relax," Lorcan said when he saw me. "We just went to get something to eat."

Teeghan came over to me and laid a kiss on my lips, instantly calming me down.

"Dinner tonight," Lorcan said. "All of us. I want justice for Peter Kennedy."

Lorcan headed inside as I slung my arm around Teeghan's shoulders and followed him in.

"Damn, babe. I never thought it possible for my brother's icy demeanor to melt. Admit it, you're a witch."

She giggled as we headed inside. She stopped dead in her tracks when she saw who Walter was tending to.

"What the fuck?"

"Relax, Teeghan," I said. "Let me explain."

"You better do it quick."

Killian was chuckling off to the side of the room, watching to see if she landed a punch on my face.

"Jeremiah didn't have any idea of the connection to you, nor did he know about Ronan's plan. He said he never would have gone along with it if he'd known. As far as we know, Jeremiah was a loose end that Ronan wanted to end."

"What do you mean?"

"Moments after we took Jeremiah out of the container to question him over a meal," I told her. "We caught Ronan on the CCTV at the docks drilling holes into the dungeon and pushing it into the harbor with our crane."

"He was trying to get rid of his own brother?" she asked, dumbfounded.

"Yes, and guess what, Jeremiah handed us some handy information," Jye said. "So I guess he's on probation with us to see what we can get."

She looked over at him and he held his hands up. "Tee, I promise you, I didn't know he would do anything to you."

"He killed my da."

Jeremiah looked down at his feet for a moment. "I know and for that, I will see him killed. Peter was nothing but a good guy to us. Especially when our dad kicked us out."

Teeghan turned to me. "I need to plan his funeral."

I nodded and made a move to follow but she held her hand up to stop me.

"I need to do it alone."

I watched as she headed up the stairs and instantly, I felt like she'd sucker punched me.

"Give it time," Killian said, putting a hand on my shoulder. "She's grieving. She'll come good and you can have your happy ever after."

He headed up the stairs to his room and I looked over at Jeremiah. Walter had finished with him but he was still very bruised.

"Do you know where he would be?" I asked him.

He shook his head. "But I do know every safe haven he has. There's also the woman he's in love with."

Instantly, I felt a jolt of excitement. "He has a lover?"

Jeremiah nodded. "A few, but there's one he trusts more than anything."

"Jye, take our new pal here and get him to pinpoint where we attack but hold off on the attack. Peter's memory needs to be preserved. No fighting until he's laid to rest."

Jye nodded and took Jeremiah into the dining room. I moved through the house and headed to my father's old study.

It was the only place I felt safe with my own thoughts and it reminded me of how calm he was, always when he looked after the family business.

He must have gone through this so many times and yet we never knew of the struggles he had.

CHAPTER SIXTEEN

CONOR

Killian smirked at me as he showed me the controller for the bomb he'd just planted. We'd been setting the bombs in each house Ronan owned, and all associates he kept. We kept a camera on each property once we set the bomb and we were going to go home and have a watch party as they blew.

One by one.

We'd left his lovers' houses alone. I didn't want him to think we knew about them. He needed to feel safe so we could rain down on him with all of our fury.

Peter's funeral was in twelve hours. Teeghan had taken a sleeping pill so she could get up early and deal with all the bullshit that came along with it.

"I've never seen you this angry before," Killian said. "I kinda like hellish Conor."

"I don't get off on it like you do," I replied. "But I know how to show my power when I need to."

Killian shrugged his shoulders. He lived for the destruction that came from all-out war whereas I used it sparingly, preferring guns and fists.

"Lorcan and Teeghan have struck up an interesting friendship."

I knew I sounded jealous, but I couldn't help it. He'd been assisting with the funeral plans for the last few days while Killian and I had been planning our attack on Ronan.

"But that's all it is. She needs a friend, not a lover. She's grieving and frankly it puts Lorcan in a better mood too. I doubt you'll need to worry about Lorcan or Teeghan in that way. She only has eyes for you."

My jealousy was something I hadn't ever had to deal with before and I didn't like it but somehow, I knew he was right. She was probably the friend Lorcan needed because fuck he was a grumpy motherfucker usually.

"Ready?" Killian asked. I nodded and he took off toward his apartment where he had the TV's set up to watch the explosions about to rock the city. Jeremiah had told us he had plenty of properties outside the city too but we'd attack them one by one, as we slowly crept toward the woman he loved.

It was time for him to feel the fire.

As Killian opened his apartment up, I sat down in front of the TV's and one by one, Killian pressed a button. Each time, the screen would change to the next property, and we'd watch it blow to smithereens.

I felt oddly justified watching them blow. That fucker had more property than I liked. How fucking rich had Murphy been to keep that much property on the downlow.

Not that it mattered anymore. The church was out of service thanks to the local priest disappearing or so the town figured. No one suspected us of mutiny on the priest everyone thought was above reproach.

Once the last house went up, Killian sat back in his chair, a huge smile on his face. He looked ten years younger.

"That was satisfying," I said with a chuckle. "Fucker knows we'll get him."

"He'll make mistakes now," Killian told me. "Then we'll get him and we'll burn this rebellion out before it can really take over."

I nodded. "I should get back to the estate. Peter's funeral is in the morning and I need to be there for Teeghan."

He nodded. "Yeah, I'll come with. She needs to know we are all here for her."

I wanted to hug him but we didn't have that kind of relationship. We were the O'Farrell's, hardened mother-fuckers who weren't to be crossed.

As I moved for the door, Killian hugged me. It was a brief one, but it meant the world to me. I nodded at him, as if silence was enough to convey how it made me feel.

"Anything for you, brother, you know that."

We headed down the driveway to Killian's car and he gunned it back to the estate. This was just the beginning.

We would rise again.

And then, everyone would know for sure that you never messed with the O'Farrell's.

THE END

Did you love Conor and Tee's story?

Why not start on Killian's story next? Will he and Sloane finally sort their issues out and make it work?

*Find out in **Killian**...*

ALSO BY KATE

A Woman Scorned Series

Mine, Forever

Havoc

The O'Farrell Brothers

Conor

Killian

Lorcan